A JOURNEY TO LOVE: KAMAYA'S STORY

MONAE NICOLE

This book is dedicated to my grandma Thomasene Wilson. I hope I'm making you proud. Continue to Rest In Peace little Tommie.

"You'll never fail if you don't take the shot."

ACKNOWLEDGMENTS

First I like to give thanks to God
To my parents for always being there for me and believing in me.
To my daughter LaShay, I'm doing this for you and to prove to you that
no matter what you can achieve everything your heart desires.
To my very own unicorn MC, thank you for encouraging me to even
write a book. If it wasn't for you I probably would have never started
this journey.
To my boo BLS, thank you for all of your encouragement and pushing
me on the days when I wanted to give up.
To my besties Shanere and Danielle, thank both of you ladies for
always being there for me.
To Zee, Saja, Krissy and Britt, thank all of you ladies for your
encouragement. #GangGang
To Annitia Jackson and Iesha Bree I can't thank you both enough for
everything y'all have done during this process. No matter how small
the question was or what time of day it was you both were always there
to answer my questions. To every other author and person that offered
words of encouragement, thank you.
To the readers, thank you for taking a chance on me. I hope you enjoy.

ONE

August, 2009

"YASS BITCH IT'S MY BIRTHDAY!", I screamed out to my best friend Tatiana, while we were getting ready to hit up club Fetish. Tonight was my 21st birthday and all I wanted to do was get some drinks, twerk a little, and turn up with my friends. Let me introduce myself, my name is Kamaya Jones and yes I am still a virgin. I know, I know, crazy right. Especially since most girls my age and in my area are thotting like it's the new norm or trend and everybody wanna be like each other. No one can be themselves anymore. My parents were married for 30 years and they taught me the importance of saving myself for marriage and that's exactly what I planned to do. Trust me when I tell you it's hard though. Now I'm not judging anyone who doesn't wait but for me at this moment I was trying to focus on my career. I just graduated college with my bachelor's in psychology and after a little break I was going back to get my master's degree, so this was a celebration for my birthday and for us just graduating college. Since before I can remember I always wanted to be a psychologist. I just find the human brain so fascinating, but enough about that let's get back to this turn up. Me, my bestie Tati, and my two friends from college Keysha and Gabrielle were all dressed to kill and we were gonna shut shit down. I'm what people would call a BBW but don't get shit twisted, I had curves in all the right places and with my Hershey chocolate skin I'm liable to take your man and your daddy, but I don't get down like that. Anyways my girls and I pulled up to the club in my black on black Range Rover that my daddy got me for graduation, and it was so crowded that the line was wrapped around the building. Finally after finding a good parking spot we made our way to the door because me and my girls don't wait in line. Keysha was messing with the bouncer so it was nothing for us to get in. Making our way to the VIP section we reserved, we kept getting stopped left and right by different dudes trying to holla at all of us.

"Girl this place is popping!, let's get some drinks", Tati said. The waitress came over and we ordered bottles of Grey Goose and Hennessy and some drinks to mix with them. I was dancing and I kept feeling someone looking at me and I think Gabi noticed too because she tapped me on my shoulder and was like "don't look now but it's a dude across from us that keeps watching you."

Trying to play it off like I didn't notice, I waited a minute before I looked again and sure enough this fine ass dude was sitting across in the other VIP section just watching me. I waved at him and just kept on dancing. Maybe about 10 minutes later I looked over and I noticed he was gone and I got a little disappointed because with this liquid courage I had from these drinks I was actually getting ready to approach him. When I looked around I saw him heading in my direction.

"Excuse me miss but I've been watching you all night and I just had to come over here and speak to you and hopefully you'll give me your phone number before this night is over."

When I first saw him from across the room I thought he was fine but baby when he got closer he looked even better. He had this nice dark chocolate skin and his smile was so perfect that my panties instantly got wet when he showed me all 32 of of his pretty ass teeth. He stood about 6 feet tall with these dark brown eyes that I just wanted to get lost in and a nice full beard and some nice juicy lips that I just wanted to suck on. My virgin mind shouldn't have been thinking like that but I couldn't help it.

"My name is Quran", he said licking his lips and snapping me out of my nasty thoughts. His Bond number 9 cologne tickled my nostrils and he smelled so good that I just wanted to stick my nose right into his neck and smell him all day.

"Um, oh my name is Kamaya", I stood there all tongue tied. He took my hand and kissed it and said it's nice to meet you. I was still standing there lusting after him but I managed to say nice meeting you too.

"So back to what I said a minute ago, do you think I can get your phone number?", as he was already handing me his phone. After I put my number in he said he was getting ready to head out and he would be calling me soon.

"Okay that's cool I told him, enjoy the rest of your night."

"You do the same sweetheart, be careful and you'll be hearing from me sooner than you think" he said and winked at me.

Watching him walk away I decided right then and there that if he did call me he would be the one I would lose my virginity to. Don't judge me, staying a virgin isn't what's it's all cracked up to be but I think it's worth waiting. "Damn who was that?, he looks familiar", Tati asked walking towards me.

"Girl that's the man that's gonna pop my cherry" I told her. I just stood there for a while fantasizing about everything I would let his fine ass do to me.

Laughing, she said "well shit I don't blame you girl because he was fine as hell!'

She was right, and if he plays his cards right he can have whatever he wants from me. For the rest of the night my girls and I continued to drink and get our party on but I couldn't get that chocolate god out of my head. I hope he really does call.

Two days later as I was on my way to the store to pick up a few items when my phone rang. "Hello," I answered.

"Good afternoon beautiful", the sound of his voice made me feel butterflies in my stomach. "Hi, Quran how are you?" I asked him. Damn he even sounded sexy over the phone.

"I'm doing good now that I hear your voice and I would be even better if you agreed to let me take you out to dinner tonight."

"Sure, I'm free tonight so I'm down." Shit either way I was going to make myself available.

"Cool, cool, well how about I pick you up around 8pm, just shoot me your address."

"Okay, I'll see you at 8." I sent him the text then I called Tati, "bitch guess who just called me", I basically shouted through the phone.

"I'm guessing that fine ass dude from the other night."

Giggling, I said "yeah girl and he wants to take me out to dinner tonight."

"Oh that's what up" she said, but the way she said it sounded a little sarcastic, if I didn't know any better she wasn't too happy about it. I just brushed it off thinking maybe she had a bad day. I feel like she's a little jealous but I'm not sure why. "Yes I'm so nervous and I don't know what to wear." This will be my first real date.

"Just put on a nice pair of jeans and a cute shirt and some heels," Tati suggested.

"Nah I think I may just wear this new little black dress I just got from this online boutique I came across a couple of weeks ago called PinkLeo boutique." They have a lot of things that most of these stores don't be selling.

"I know, I just ordered something from there myself a couple days ago."

"Anyway girl let me get ready for this date because he should be here in about two hours and I need to get myself together."

"Okay, call me and let me know how it goes and don't do anything I wouldn't do," Tati said before she hung up.

At exactly 8pm my doorbell rang and when I opened the door and found Quran standing there looking better than he did the other night I didn't even know what to say. His outfit was simple but he made it look good as hell. He was wearing an orange shirt which looked nice against his smooth chocolate skin with some jeans and some black and orange air maxes.

"Wow you look beautiful." When he smiled at me I noticed how white his teeth were. It was like they were sparkling.

"Thank you, you don't look too bad yourself," I responded back. "I'm all ready to go," he grabbed my keys from me and locked the door for me.

When he put his hand on the small of my back to guide me down the stairs I felt a chill go up my spine. If a simple touch like that was so electrifying than I can only imagine what a kiss or more intimate touching would do to me. He opened the car door for me and then we were off to wherever he was taking me. About twenty minutes later we arrived at Ruth Chris steakhouse, I was low key excited because I had never been here before but I didn't show it.

"So... Miss Kamaya tell me about yourself." I liked the fact that while he was talking he was giving me direct eye contact.

"Well I just turned 21, I recently graduated from college with a bachelor's degree in psychology. I really want to get my masters, then doctorate to become a psychologist. I really like looking into people's minds as well help people get through everyday issues in life. In my spare time I like to read and just hang out with my girls."

The whole time I was talking he seemed to be really interested in what I had to say.

"How about yourself?"

"I'm 22 and I also just graduated from college with a bachelors in engineering. I'm looking to become an electrical engineer, but I want to get my masters degree first. In my spare time I like to play basketball with my boys or relax with a good book. There is nothing like a good book to escape into for a couple of hours."

"Oh a reader, that's interesting. What type of books do you like to read?"

"I read a lot of Donald Goines and Iceberg Slim books, but I also like James Patterson, and I also love Marvel comics. What type of books are you into?"

"Well I also like Donald Goines and Iceberg Slim but I also like Terri McMillan. Some street but also some romance, and I definitely love Marvel comics."

"What would be your favorite Donald Goines book? Mine is Whoreson." I asked, he definitely had all of my attention.

"Oh shit that's mine too! See we're already starting off with something in common." "So tell me Miss Kamaya what are you looking for in a man?"

"Probably the same thing most women want, trust, communication, loyalty, you know, someone I can build a future with, maybe get married and have a couple of children with. I'm not a complicated girl, I just like to live life, laugh, and spend time with my loved ones. Sometimes I just like to be left alone, nothing personal but I think everyone needs some alone time, especially in relationships. You have to be able to do things together and apart or the relationship becomes stagnant quickly."

"Yeah I pretty much feel the same way as you. Your pretty sure of what you want at such a young age, I think that's a good thing."

"My mother always told me I had an old soul," I said with a light chuckle. After that we just continued to eat and just talked about all types of stuff from politics to movies and music. The conversation just flowed naturally and he made me feel really comfortable. It was like we've known each other for a while even though we didn't. Once we were done with dinner we decided to take a walk in the nearby park. He grabbed my hand and it just felt so natural. It was nice just strolling along and getting to know each other.

TWO

THINGS WITH QURAN the last couple of weeks have been going pretty well. We talk every single day and we have been out on a few dates since the first night. Tonight is another date night for us. As I was getting dressed I noticed Tati calling me.

"Hello,"

"Hey Kam, what you up to?"

"Not much, what you up to?"

"Oh girl I'm just getting ready for this date with Quran."

"Another one, you must really like him huh?"

I sensed a little hint of jealousy when she asked. "Yes I do really like him, I mean I'm not talking about marriage or babies or anything like that but I'm definitely feeling him. He's a nice guy with a good head on his shoulders and he has real plans for his future."

"Well I was calling to see if you wanted to hang out but your busy so I'll just try another day," she said sadly.

"Aww boo I promise we will hang out sometime soon. How about we hit something up this weekend, we can make up a whole day out of it. We can get our nails and feet done, have dinner and maybe hit up club Fetish again," I suggested.

"Okay that's cool, well enjoy yourself and I'll talk to you soon."

I hung up with her and continued to get dressed, Tonight we were going to Lucky Strike to go bowling, probably eat and have a couple of drinks. I kept my outfit simple with a pair of skinny jeans and a Biggie Smalls t-shirt, and a pair of black air maxes. My makeup only consisted of some mac lip gloss but I added some simple jewelry and was all set to go. The doorbell rang, and I went down to answer because I knew it was Quran. When I opened the door he was standing there smiling at me and I got those butterflies in my stomach again. This happened every time he came around.

"Hello beautiful," he said to me, licking his lips again. I noticed he does that a lot.

"Hey handsome how are you?"

"I'm doing good now that I get to see your beautiful face." I just started blushing and told him I was ready to go.

We arrived at Lucky Strike and got something to eat first and had a few drinks. By the time we started bowling, I had already had about 3 drinks so I was feeling a little tipsy. As he was getting ready to roll the ball, I whispered in his ear that I wanted him to take my virginity. He was so surprised that he damn near dropped the ball on his foot.

We both looked at each other and laughed and then he turned to me with a serious face and said to me, "babygirl as much as I would love to put this dick in your life, I don't think your ready just yet but trust me when the time is right it will change your life," he smacked me on my ass and turned to walk away.

I just stood there and looked at him for a minute because I wasn't sure how to respond to that, after a few seconds I just said um okay. He gave me that sexy ass smile again and continued to bowl. I just sat there and admired the fact that he just didn't jump at the opportunity to have sex with me and chose to wait. Some of these other niggas would have ran up out of there trying to fuck a virgin.

"I would rather you be my girl first before we take it there because once we do sweetheart there is no going back."

"So Miss Kamaya would you like to be my girlfriend?" It took me no time to think about it. I really liked him and I think we have a good vibe and we both want the same things out of life so why not.

"Yes I would love to be your girlfriend and thank you for suggesting we wait to have sex." I think those couple of drinks had me feeling bold. So from that night forward Quran and I became a couple and I was excited to see where things were headed with us.

Finally Saturday had arrived and I was going to hang out with my girls. Tati and I were going to get manicures and pedicures, then meet up with Gabi and Keysha at my house so we can pregame before we hit up the club. "So Tati what's been going on with you," I asked while we were sitting there getting our feet done.

"Girl you know me same old shit, just getting ready for school to start back up soon." Like me Tati decided to go back to school to get her master's degree.

"Yeah I hear that, I'm getting ready for it myself. Well in other news, Quran and I decided to make things official."

"Damn already you haven't known him that long."

"No I haven't but I like the vibe we have and I'm willing to take a chance on him."

"Well have you told him your a virgin?" she asked me like that was supposed to make a difference in things.

"As a matter of fact yes I did tell him and I told him I wanted him to take my virginity and he said he would but he doesn't think that I'm ready yet. To be honest I'm kinda not ready but I know I want it to be with him."

"Hmm, well I still think it's kinda early but whatever."

"As my best friend I thought you would be happy for me."

"It's not that I'm not happy, but I just think you may be moving too fast."

I sat there thinking about what she said and maybe she was right but a part of me felt like she was a little jealous. "Anyway, let's get ready to get out of here so we can eat something before we head to my house."

We all met up at my house to have some drinks and to get ready for the club.

"So Kam what's up with you and that fine ass dude from the club that night?" Gabi asked me.

"I'm happy to say that he is now my boyfriend and I'm ready to let him be my first," I gushed.

"Oh wow, I'm happy for you and tell him if he doesn't act right I will kick his ass."

"I sure will tell him," I said laughing. I looked over at Tati and I noticed her rolling her eyes and she always has something negative to say when I bring him up so I couldn't let that shit slide no more. "Tati do you have something you want to get off your chest? It's like every time I bring up Quran you have something negative to say. "Nope I sure don't, I just want you to be careful Kam." I wasn't convinced by her response but I was gonna let it go for now.

A couple of hours later we were in line at club Fetish. Once again we didn't have to wait in line because Keysha was still messing with the bouncer. 'Independent' by Webbie was playing and we went straight to the dance floor.

"This my shit" I yelled while shaking my ass. Suddenly some chick bumped into me, "excuse you bitch you wanna watch where you going!"

"Oh my bad, shit not really, but uh do you mess with Quran? I saw y'all at Lucky Strike a couple of days ago."

"Yeah I do, why the fuck you worried about it?"

"Well I'm just letting you know that he's my man so I suggest you leave him alone."

"Oh ya man huh, so why the fuck you didn't say shit when you saw us huh? Instead you wait until I'm not with him because you know Quran would have shut ya dumb ass down. Fuck outta my face with this shit." I said shooing her away. She got me fucked up if she thinks I believe her dumb ass. Yea Quran and I just got together, so he could have been with her without me knowing. However, if he was her man as she says she should have approached us when we were together.

"I decided to let y'all live that night but I'm telling you now bitch!" she had the nerve to say.

"Here's what we not gone do is call me anything other than my name and since you don't know my name there is no need for you to be talking to me at all."

"Well bitch like I said you need to leave Qu.." before she can even get his whole name out I punched that bitch right in her mouth. I'm not about to be fighting over no dude but I refused to be disrespected.

At that point I started whooping her ass and I dared her friends to jump in it. After a good three minutes security came and broke up the fight. That bitch was laying there with blood coming out of her nose and her eye was already starting to swell. "Now if you want me to leave Quran alone, you tell him to tell me that!" I spat and walked off.

After the bullshit I was ready to get out of there. I was just trying to enjoy my night with my girls but some bitch had to come at me with some bullshit. As soon as we stepped outside Tati started with her shit.

"See I told you that you were moving too fast with him." In my mind I'm thinking shut the hell up but I didn't say anything because I didn't want to fight with her ass either. At this point anybody is liable to catch these hands.

"Girl just because some random ass girl said some bullshit about being with him doesn't mean it's true," Keysha said. "Shit it could just be some bitch he used to fuck with and don't want anymore or she could just want to fuck with him and he didn't want to. Like really think about, if she was that important then she would have approached y'all when she saw y'all together."

"She has a point there," Gabi said.

"Well I still think he may be up to something," Tati said. Of course she did.

"Well the only way to find out is to ask him myself which I will do when I get home."

"Hmph, do you think he's going to tell you the truth?"

"Yes Tati I do believe he will, there is no reason to lie about anything."

"I guess so," she said with an attitude, while rolling her eyes.

I was just over this whole night so I chose not to even respond to her anymore and just drove off so they can get their cars from my house and I can call Quran. As soon as we got to my house I said goodnight to them and went to call his ass.

THREE

"WHAT'S UP MA?"

"Hey, let me cut to the chase, some chick came up to me in the club and insisted that I stop messing with you because y'all were together. She said she saw us at Lucky Strike but decided not to say anything. I had to whoop her ass for talking reckless and now I'm asking you if what she said is true because I don't have play second to no one."

"Did you get shorty name?"

"Yeah the bitch name was Tasha or some shit."

"Well sweetheart the only Tasha I know is some bitch I used to fuck with a minute ago before I met you but I cut her off after you and I started talking so I guess she got mad that I stopped fucking with her. You don't have to worry about her or any of these other broads out here, it's just me and you baby."

A part of me didn't believe him but he hasn't giving me any reason to think otherwise so I decided to throw caution to the wind and keep pushing forward in the relationship.

"Okay but here's the thing, shouldn't no bitch have the balls to think she can come to me like that about you. So if the shit happens again you and the bitch will be floating in the Delaware river."

"Haha, I hear you baby," he chuckled.

"I'm deadass though Quran, I don't have time to be playing no childish ass games."

"I got you ma. So anyway beautiful what you going on?"

"Not much I just came back from the club and getting ready to take my ass to bed, school starts on Monday so I'm just trying to relax and get myself ready for this hard ass semester."

"Yeah I hear that, I have to get ready for it myself. Go head and get your beauty rest and I'll talk you tomorrow."

"Okay goodnight." Once I hung up with him I called Tati to let her know that Quran and I talked and everything is all good. To be honest I don't even know why I was calling her hating ass but I did anyway. Calling her phone I thought she wasn't going to answer because it just kept ringing, "hey girl she said all out of breath."

"Uh hey, are you okay it sounds like you can barely breathe."

"Oh girl I'm good, was a little occupied, but anyway what's up?"

"Well I was just calling to let you know about the conversation Quran and I had, he said that girl was some chick he used to fuck with but he cut off her and I guess she mad now."

"Mmmhmm, of course he gonna say that. Shit he may be lying."

"Tati you just won't cut him a break huh, it's like you don't have any faith that I can find a good dude."

"No it's not that Kam, it's just that I know how these niggas are out here and I don't want you getting hurt."

"Well he hasn't giving me any reason to think otherwise so I'm going to believe him."

"Okay just be careful boo."

"Don't worry bestie, I'm being careful. Well I'm about to get ready for bed, I'll talk to you later." I couldn't deal with her negativity anymore.

Once Quran and I got that little situation handled things have been going great for us. We have been going out on more dates and we have talked about building a future together. We still haven't had sex but we have kissed a lot and baby those lips of his are like little pillows. Everytime he kisses me or even touches me I get a chill up my spine. I'm appreciative of him being patient with me and I think I'm going to reward him tonight. We were going to have dinner and come back to my place to watch a movie and just chill out. With both of us in school full time our time is limited so we have to make the best out of our date nights. Tonight we had dinner at Fogo De Chao and now we are at my house getting ready to watch Iron Man on DVD, even though we saw it already.

"Would you like something to drink?"

"Nah sweetheart I'm good"

"Okay, well let me go slip on something more comfortable and I'll be right back."

"No problem, do you want me to start the movie or wait for you."

"No you can start, it won't take me long."

Standing in my mirror I had to give myself a pep talk, I was so nervous. I had on this red one piece lingerie outfit I got from Fredericks of Hollywood with some six inch heels. I stood in the mirror talking to myself. You got this girl, so calm down. I was very confident in myself but this is the first time someone would see me like this and my first time having sex, if it happens. If he didn't want to fuck me after seeing me like this then either he really doesn't like me or his ass is gay, and I don't believe either one.

When I walked back into the living room he was so into the movie that he didn't even notice me. Ahem, I cleared my throat then he finally saw me.

Damn, was all he said and the look he gave me made me feel hot all over. "Why you standing so far away?, come here girl" he said motioning me with his index finger.

I walked slowly over to him so he can fully see my outfit and because I was nervous as hell. As soon as I got in front of him he lifted my thick ass up and placed me on his lap.

"Damn baby this all for me?," he asked while rubbing my ass. Shly I said yes it is as he started to kiss on my neck, and that gave me chills. Then he grabbed me holding both sides of my face and kissed me like he never kissed me before. This kiss was passionate, it was like he was making love to my mouth.

In between kisses he managed to whisper, can we take this to your bedroom. I was so hot and bothered that all I can do was nod my head. He lifted me and himself off the couch and walked us back to my room still kissing me. Laying me down on my bed he began rubbing all over my body, and it felt so good.

"Can I taste it baby?" He asked me in this low seductive voice that made my pussy jump.

"Yes you can," I panted, he slowly started kissing me down my body from my neck to my breast then he sucked on each of my nipples, then my stomach and finally when he reached my pussy he started out with soft, tiny kisses but when his soft wet tongue licked my clit I damn near lost my mind. He was down there feasting on my pussy like it was his last meal. After a minute or two I started to feel this pressure build up in my stomach and didn't know what was happening.

He then stuck a finger in me while he was still licking and said "I feel it baby let it out." When he said that I lost all control and I came all in his mouth, and he didn't let a drop go to waste. Once he came up he kissed me again letting me taste my own juices then he pulled out his dick and my damn eyes popped out of my head. There was no way in hell that thing was going in me.

He must of noticed my apprehension because he chuckled and said "don't worry baby it's only going to hurt a little," and he had the nerve to wink his damn eye. Once he put a condom on, he laid on top of me and kissed me again, slowly inching his dick in me.

Shit, he grunted in my ear, your pussy is so wet and tight. I'm glad you saved it for me baby. I couldn't even get any words out so I just moaned in response to what he said. I felt another orgasm and he must have felt it too because he started to speed up and he was like yes baby wet that dick up and I did just that. A couple strokes later he came too.

For the rest of the night he flipped and turned my fat ass in ways I didn't even know my body can move. After that night I think I fell in love with Quran Green.

FOUR

Six Months Later...

FOR THE LAST six months things with Quran and I have been wonderful. We spend time together pretty much everyday and we go on weekly dates to try to keep things fresh with us. The sex is off the chain but considering he's the only person I had sex with, of course it was for me. Everyday he sends me good morning and goodnight texts as well as texting me throughout the day and brings me lunch when he can. We are friends as well as lovers and I couldn't ask for a better boyfriend.

I have noticed that Tati has been becoming a little distant and I'm not sure why. Just because I have a boyfriend doesn't mean that I don't have time with my friends. Trying to juggle school, a boyfriend, and my friends has been hard but I'm doing the best I can. I'll call Tati and see if she wants to hang out just me and her so we can catch up. Lately I've been feeling real tired and moody all the time and my period is 2 months late. Quran and I haven't really talked about having children since we both are still in school full time so I'm not sure how he will feel if I really am pregnant. Maybe I should take a test before I jump the gun.

Let me call Tati and invite her to lunch so I can talk to her about it and maybe she can be there when I take the test. Grabbing my phone from the table I dialed her number.

"Hey Tati how are you?"

"Hey girl I'm doing good, how are things with you?"

"I'm good. I was wondering if you wanted to meet up for lunch today so we can catch up, if feels like I haven't seen you in a while."

"Yeah because you haven't" she said sarcastically, "your always with your boyfriend and don't have time for me anymore."

"Boo that is not true so don't even try it, I chuckled. Anyway do you want to meet at Applebee's around 12:30?"

"Yeah, I'll just meet you there."

"Cool, see you in a little bit" I said before I hung up the phone.

Arriving at Applebee's found a parking spot right next to Tati and we both got out of our cars at the same time. Walking over to her I reached out to hug her.

"Hey boo, you look cute" I said to her then kissed her cheek. She had on this light pink sweater dress with some cute knee boots.

"Thanks girl, you look cute yourself." I was wearing a black sweater dress with some black ankle boots.

We went inside and immediately got seated. Since it was hardly anybody in there the waiter came right over and we placed our orders. I ordered the bourbon street chicken and shrimp and a strawberry lemonade and Tati ordered the firecracker shrimp cavatappi and an apple martini. We pretty much got the same thing everytime we came here.

"So Kam what's being going with you," she asked me as soon as the waiter walked away.

"Well, I said with a deep sigh, I think I may be pregnant."

"Oh wow, I didn't expect you to say that, what's make you think that?"

I paused because the waiter came over with our food, taking a sip of my drink I responded, "well because I'm always tired, I've been really moody and my period is late."

"Have you talked to Quran about it?"

"No I'll wait until after I take the test. Will you come to my house after we leave here and be there with me?"

"Sure we're besties so of course I will be there."

Once we leave here I need to stop at CVS to grab a couple of test then I'll meet you at my place. After leaving CVS I met Tati at my place, since she had a key she already was inside. Well here goes nothing I said to her as I walked to the bathroom. I peed on the stick at waited like 10 minutes because I was so nervous. Finally looking at the test it said clear as day I was definitely pregnant.

I went into the living room and Tati was anxious, "so are you pregnant or not?"

"Yup I'm pregnant and I'm not sure if Quran is going to be happy or not, it's still kind of early to be having a baby."

"Congratulations!," she hesitated while hugging me and smiling but the smile didn't reach her eyes. I really feel like my own best friend doesn't want me happy or to be with Quran but I don't understand why. "Tati, are you not happy with me being with Quran and now being pregnant by him?"

"Of course I am girl, why would you ask me that?"

"I don't know Tati it just seems like whenever I talk about him you have this weird look on your face or make these sarcastic remarks."

"Girl I just have alot on my mind, it has nothing to do with you," she tried telling me but I'm still not convinced and I'm not going to worry about it.

"Well just know that I'm always here for you."

"I know girl and I appreciate you. Well I'm going to get ready to go," she told me.

"Thanks for coming over here and doing this with me, let me call Quran and let him know he's going to be a father." I couldn't let her negative energy get me down.

FIVE

I SAT NERVOUSLY on my couch waiting for Quran to come over. I called him like a hour ago to tell him we had to talk. I was in deep thought about being a mother and how he was going to react that the knocking at my door scared the shit out of me. Jumping up, I ran to the door. When I opened the door he was standing with just a plain white tee and some jeans on with that smile that makes me weak every time.

"What's up beautiful?" he said as he kissed me on my lips.

"Hey baby, how was your day?" I asked while making room for him to sit down.

"It was busy but it was good, how was yours?" he asked me.

"Well it was good, I had lunch with Tatiana and found out something interesting and that's why I called you over." He gave me the side eye probably thinking it was some bullshit. He ran his hand over his waves and looked at me while licking his lips. Every time he does that I lose my train of thought but this was important so I had to get it together. I took a deep breath and blurted out "I'm pregnant!" He just stared at me intensely for like 30 seconds before he started smiling.

"Seriously baby, your having my baby, I'm really going to be a father?" he asked excitedly.

"Yes we are having a baby! Do you think we are ready for a baby though?"

"Honestly sweetheart we probably aren't but is anybody ever really ready for a baby? Besides there is nobody I would rather have a baby with than you."

"Good because I feel the same way, I love you Quran."

"I love you too baby girl."

Next thing I know he picked me up and started kissing me and before I knew it my dress was on the floor. As he sat down on the couch he placed me in front of him with just my bra and panties on. He started kissing on my stomach and told me he loved me and that he was happy I was having his baby. Then he pulled down my panties and started kissing his way down from my stomach down to my freshly shaved pussy. When he started sucking on my clit my damn legs almost gave out. After a couple more minutes he laid me on the couch and continued feasting. "Yes baby right there I moaned out." Right before I was getting ready to cum he stopped, then he came up and slid his dick in me nice and slow. No matter how many times we have sex it always feels like the first. He lifted my leg and put it on his shoulder and continued to give me deep slow strokes. I guess he knew I was cumming and he probably was too because he started to speed up his pace.

"Oooh, harder baby, harder" I screamed out.

"Damn girl this pussy is extra wet tonight he grunted, I'm about to cum, are you going to cum with me?" he asked.

"Yes baby," I moaned, after about three more strokes we came at the same time. Trying to catch my breath I said I love you Quran.

"I love you too beautiful," and we both passed out right on the couch.

For the last couple of months this baby has been kicking my ass but I've still been going to school and Quran has been taking care of me and catering to my needs. From the food cravings to rubbing my feet and back whenever I wanted him too. Like right now we were sitting on my couch while he was giving me the best foot massage.

"So baby girl are you hoping for a boy or girl?"

"Honestly I just want a healthy baby, why what do you want it to be?"

He smirked at me, "well you know I need a junior but I'll be happy with either one."

"I'm not sure I can deal with another you," he said to me.

I threw a pillow at him, "I'm not that bad" I said.

He stopped massaging my foot and looked me at all crazy, "says who? Babygirl your spoiled and stubborn and I know if we have a girl she's going to be just like you."

"Well hopefully we can find out tomorrow when we go for my appointment," I said to him.

"Yes baby I know so we should get some rest so we will be on time," he suggested. He was staying the night since my appointment was in the morning and my place was closer to my doctor's office than his was.

The next day we got up, and had breakfast at IHOP then went to my appointment. I was excited because we were finally going to be able to find out what we were having. I checked in at the front desk and within minutes they called us back to the room. I got comfortable on the exam table and Quran sat right next to me holding my hand. After about five minutes Dr. Ferguson came in, "how's mommy and daddy doing today?"

"Good!" we both said at the same time and laughed. "I bet you guys want to see what your having?" she asked us.

"Yes we do!" We both answered.

"Okay Kam lay back for me and let's see what we can find out." She rubbed the cold gel on my stomach and we heard our baby's heartbeat, it was such a surreal moment that I began crying. I've never heard something so beautiful in my life. After she moved the ultrasound thing around a little she told us we were having a girl.

"Oh lord I better get my gun now" Quran said laughing.

"Don't be so dramatic bae" I giggled.

"If she's anything like her pretty ass mom then I'm gonna have to shoot these little knuckleheads."

He always says things to make blush, well not the shooting part but about me being pretty. Dr. Ferguson printed out a couple of pictures for us and we went to enjoy the rest of our day together since neither one of us had class today.

December 2009

My due date was finally approaching and I couldn't wait to finally be able to meet my baby girl. I had signed up for online classes so I can still attend school and stay home with the baby. Lately I have just been getting my place together and trying to get as much sleep as I can because I know once this baby comes there is no more rest happening. Quran has practically moved in and we just got the nursery together. Today I was going to get mani's and pedi's with my girls. That way when the baby comes I'll still be fly. I met the girls at the nail shop and caught up with them since I didn't see them in a couple of weeks.

"Girl this feels so good," I said to them while we were sitting in the massage chairs getting our pedicures done.

"I know right," Keysha said.

"Are you ready for the baby?" Gabi asked.

"Yes I can't wait to meet my princess. My feet are swollen, my back hurts, I'm peeing all the time, and I can't ever get comfortable, so I'm definitely ready."

After about two hours of getting pampered we all headed out but before we could get anywhere I felt this gush of fluid running down my legs. "Uh guys, I think my water just broke."

"Oh shit!, we have to get you to the hospital!"

Shit, the pain shot through me before I was able to get in the car. "Wait I have to call Quran" I screamed out. There was no way I was having this baby without him being there.

"Okay Kam try to get into the car first then we'll call" I slowly eased my way in, then I grabbed my phone out of my bag. He answered after a couple rings, "bae the baby's coming, Ughh!" I screamed in his ear.

"Okay beautiful I'll meet you at the hospital, just breathe baby." About ten minutes later we arrived at the hospital and Gabi ran inside to get some help and they came out with a wheelchair. They wheeled me to a room and they helped me to the bed. A couple minutes later Quran came in and right behind him was Dr. Ferguson.

"Ms. Jones I am gonna examine you and see how many centimeters your dilated." She told me I was about 5 centimeters then she told me she would be back in a little while.

About three hours later I was ready to push this baby out. The girls were out in the waiting room so it was just Quran in there with me. "Kam on the count of 3 I want you to push, 1,2,3, push" Ughhh! I yelled. Take another deep breath and push on the count of three one more time, 1,2,3 push. Ughh, I pushed so hard but then I heard the sweet sound of my baby crying. Congratulations its a girl, and on December 23, 2009, I gave birth to my baby girl Summer Reign Green.

SIX

THINGS for the last two months have been great. Being a mother wasn't something that I imagined I would be doing at this age but I was definitely enjoying it. Quran has been such a wonderful father to our baby. We always would take turns getting up in the middle of the night when she wakes up. Everything is perfect and I couldn't ask for a better boyfriend or father for my daughter.

We finally would be getting time for each other tonight since my parents wanted Summer for the night. This would be the first time away from her for so long but Quran and I needed it. It's been hard for us to have any real alone time lately so I was looking forward to it. He told me he had a surprise for me so I had no idea where we were going.

While Summer was sleep I got up to clean the house a little and get myself ready for date night. I also had to get some school work done. I'll be lucky if I get a little nap in somewhere too. Luckily I got everything thing done and was able to lay down for a little bit. I woke up about a hour later and I went to go check on Summer in the nursery and Quran was in there holding her in the rocking chair.

I stood there and watched them for a little bit. I couldn't believe I was so lucky to have such a beautiful baby and a great man. He must have felt my presence because he stopped rocking and looked up at me and smiled.

"Kam baby don't be standing there all creepy and shit just staring at me", he chuckled. "Boy please wasn't nobody staring at your ugly ass" I said while walking over to him.

"Shorty you and I both know I ain't ugly so don't even try it. Anyway baby mamma you ready for our date tonight?"

"Yes baby I'm ready and I can't wait to see where you are taking me."

"Good, now get your sexy ass ready." he said and smacked me on my ass.

A hour and a half later we both were ready to go. After getting Summer ready we were headed to my parents to drop her off and go wherever he was taking me since I still had no idea as to where we were going, I strapped the baby in and we were on our way. I like surprises so I was super excited.

After dropping Summer off we ended going to the train station and I kept asking where we were going but he still wouldn't tell me. I was hoping we weren't going to be outside because it's still cold as hell out and I hate the cold. You would think living in New Jersey all my life that I would be used to the cold but nah I hate it. Quran found a place for us to park and we were headed to the train platform. "Babe are you going to tell me where we are going now?" I asked him while kissing his soft ass lips. "Nope not telling you but here comes the train so you will find out soon." We got on the train and about a hour later we ended up in New York.

I have been to New York plenty of times but no matter how much I come here I still get excited. It was just something about the bright lights and the people that made it fun to me. I was so excited to be here I just kept talking and talking. Our first stop was Dallas BBQ. Every time I come to the city I have to come and eat here. They have thee best chicken wings I ever ate. We sat there and ate for a little bit and had a couple of drinks.

After we ate we ended up going in Toys R Us and we got on the Ferris wheel and picked up a couple of things for Summer. The last and final stop was the ice skating rink. I was too damn nervous to try it but I didn't want to tell Quran that.

"Come on baby let me see what you got" he said to me grabbing my hand.

"Um I ain't got shit because I've never ice skated before, and I don't think I want to try now." "For real?" he questioned like it was something normal for black people to do. Maybe for some but definitely not for me. "Yes I'm for real, hell I barely can skate." I chuckled. "Well don't worry baby I promise I got you and I won't let you fall." After I thought about it for a few seconds I decided to say forget it and give it a shot. "Aight don't let me fall Quran" I told him rolling my eyes. He just laughed at me and grabbed my hand and we walked towards the rink.

It took me a few tries but I finally got the hang of it. I fell a couple of times and even made Quran fall a couple of times too but I still was having fun. I really wish I would have tried this a long time ago.

We just skated around for a little bit when suddenly Quran stopped me and got down on one knee. I was so surprised I just started crying.

"Kamaya since we've been together you have made me the happiest I have ever been and you blessed me with my first daughter and I can't thank you enough for her. I want to spend the rest of my life with you so would you do me the honor of becoming my wife?" In his hand he had a simple princess cut diamond ring. I really couldn't believe he was proposing to me right now. "Yes Quran I will marry you" He got up and kissed me while everyone around us was applauding. This had to be one of the happiest days of my life.

SEVEN

Two Years Later...

THESE PAST TWO years have been a whirlwind. My baby girl was getting so big and I was getting ready to graduate college with my master's. Switching over to online classes made it possible for me to stay on track. Quran is also about to graduate as well. Speaking of him, things have been a little rocky with us lately. I'm not sure what's been going on but I've been feeling like he may be cheating on me. Lately he's been coming home later and later. I notice him sometimes texting more on his phone than he ever has before. We barely even have sex anymore. I know for a while I wasn't the same but it was so hard having a baby and trying to finish school. I feel like he didn't understand how I was feeling and he didn't even try. I really hoped he would talk to me if there was a serious problem going on.

I wanted to pick up a few things because I wanted to plan something special for Quran to try and get us back on track. Now I left him home with the baby so imagine my surprise when I came home and saw a very familiar looking car parked at my house.

Slowly walking into my house I hear Trey Songz singing "Jupiter Love" coming from my room. Smiling because my fiancé must have took heed to the heart to heart we had the other day. In regards to the direction our relationship was going. Quran and I have been together for 2 years, and in the beginning everything was great. He used to treat me like the Queen I am, but lately I have been feeling like a peasant, beneath him. Walking up the stairs, I could have sworn I heard what sounded like a woman moaning. Now I know I must be tripping because there is no way I should be hearing another woman in my room, in my house. The house that I pay the majority of the bills in & where my 2 year old daughter resides.

As I approach the door I hear "ooh, yes daddy right there." Busting through the door I see my best friend Tatiana and my fiancé Quran fucking in my bed!

"What the fuck!"

"Baby this isn't what it looks like," he replied jumping up from the bed.

"Well to me it looks like your fucking my best friend in my bed, in my damn house with my daughter in the next room." I felt like I was having an outer body experience, this really couldn't be happening.

"Kamaya I'm so sorry, I didn't mean for this to happen," Tatiana said to me.

"Yeah whatever bitch, so let me guess you just slipped and fell on his dick?" I laughed because both of these fools think I'm crazy. And to make it so bad he was fucking this bitch raw!

You nasty mother fucker, you in here fucking this bitch raw?" Nah, I just know I wasn't seeing that shit.

Walking around my room trying to gather some stuff because I had to get out of there before I killed them both. When I walked into the closet I noticed all his clothes and those damn Jordan's that he loved so much and decided they all needed a little bleach bath, so I took all the shit I could grab and walked out headed to the bathroom and threw all of it in the tub and poured a whole damn bottle of bleach on them. My damn eyes started burning but fuck this nigga and all his shit.

Quran comes running in, "Kam what the fuck are you doing?" You bugging ma, we can work this shit out.

"Work it out!?" I shouted with tears coming down my face. I started punching him all over, the face, back, arms, wherever the hell my hands could reach. "Nigga you just raw dogged my best friend how the fuck are we going to work this out?"

Turning to leave out the room, Tatiana stops me.

"Kamaya wait just let me explain what happened. I came over here to talk to you because my grandma died today. I was crying and Quran tried to comfort me and one thing led to another and it just happened."

"It just happened? So you used your grandmother's death to fuck my man? How long has this shit really been going on with y'all? I've seen y'all looking at each other a little funny sometimes but I tried to ignore it because I thought there is no way in hell the two most important people can do me like that, boy was I wrong," I blurted. "To be honest with you though Kamaya, I actually saw him first way before he approached you in the club." I know this bitch wasn't sitting here telling me this like it's gonna make a difference. "Well Tatiana as my friend, best friend at that you should have told me that from the beginning, not let me talk to him, have a baby, and get engaged to him. The night we saw him at the club you should have something.

"I'm not gonna lie Kam when he was coming our way I thought he was coming to talk to me not you, so imagine my surprise when he approached you instead." Oh so now she wants to act like someone couldn't pass her up to talk to me. I felt like that was low blow. Next thing I know I just blacked out and starting beating this bitch ass. "Bitch..I..thought..we..were..friends! fucking had your back whenever you needed me and this is the thanks I get." I felt Quran trying to pull me off of her.

"Baby please don't go," Quran begged. "I promise it won't happen again."

Laughing, I said "I told you from the beginning don't play with me and what the fuck you do, play me, with me best friend at that! You lucky I don't send you and this bitch floating I'm done with ya lying, trifling ass. I'm taking my baby to a hotel and when I come back tomorrow I want you and Tatiana out of my house, bitch don't ever in your life call me again, pretend you don't even know me bitch because this friendship is over!" I said as I kicked that bitch in the head on the way out.

EIGHT

I wish i could believe you, then I'd be alright
But now everything you told me really don't apply to the
way i feel inside
Loving you was easy once upon a time
But now my suspicions of you have multiplied
And it's all because you lied

THESE WORDS SPOKE to my soul as I played Resentment by Beyoncé over and over. Every few minutes I sat there crying my eyes out and now my head hurts and my damn eyes are red and puffy as hell. Like how can two of the most important people in my life do me like that. I know things haven't been the same with me and him but damn my best friend.

And that bitch can't justify the shit no matter how hard she tried. I mean we've been friends since fucking kindergarten and this the shit she pulls. Shit with friends like her who the hell needs enemies.

For the last week they both keep calling me and I wasn't going to answer for either one of them but I guess I had to talk to Quran sooner or later since we had a child together. Tati on the other hand, I didn't have shit to say to that trifling bitch. The only thing I've been doing is crying and questioning everything. Like what did I do so wrong for him to fuck with my best friend of all people. No matter how much I thought about it I couldn't come up with a reason good enough for them to be this fucking foul. This shit is pissing me off all over again. I go from crying to anger then back to crying. I just want this fucking pain to stop.

Speaking of Quran he's calling me yet again. "What do you want Quran?"

"Kam I just want to talk to you and apologize, can I come over."

This nigga think he slick trying to come over knowing the baby ain't here. I bet you he going to try and get in my draws, not today Satan! "Hell no! The baby isn't here so there is no need you for you to be here."

"Come on Kam why are you being like this, I just need a few minutes of your time and I'll go about my business."

"Fine Quran, you can come by for minute to talk."

"Cool, thank you, I'll see you in about 30 minutes."

While waiting for Quran to come I decided to get up and shower and get dressed since I have just been laying in bed for the last couple of days. After showering and throwing on some shorts and a tank top

I felt so much better. As soon as I finished putting my hair up in a bun I heard my doorbell ring.

When I opened the door I couldn't deny how good he looked even though it looked like he needed a shape up, he was standing there looking fuckable. He smiled at me and I had to get my thoughts together before I messed around and had him in my bed instead of talking. Opening the door wider to let him come in the smell of his cologne tickled my nostrils and I let out a low moan. I know he put that shit on on purpose thinking it was going to change my mind, nah not happening. Clearing my throat I said "okay you're here now so speak'"

"Kam listen to me baby I didn't mean for it to happen, it was like stuff was going on with us, we've barely been fucking and she was coming onto me and it just happened."

"So because I have been taking care of your child and trying to finish school to secure a future for our family you decide to fuck my best friend! This is all my fault huh, you couldn't just keep your dick in your pants!" His ass making me upset all over again, I felt the tears but I refused to let them fall in front of him.

"That's not what I'm saying Kam, look I fucked up but I don't want to lose my family."

"You should have thought about that before you stuck ya little dick in my best friend.

"First of all Kam my dick ain't little but that's besides the point. I can promise you sweetheart it will never happen again."

"It's not like I haven't heard that before." See in the beginning of our relationship Quran slipped up and fucked some chick he used to mess with but I didn't trip off it at the time because we were only together for like two weeks at that time. I should have known though sooner or later he was going to mess things up but not with my best friend though. I'm getting mad all over again just thinking about it.

"I really mean it this time Kam, I won't do no shit like that ever again. I'll do whatever it takes to make things right. Please forgive me."

"I know it won't because I am done with ya nasty dick ass." He looked at me with pleading eyes, looking all sexy but I quickly opened the door and put his ass out before he managed to talk me out of my panties.

NINE

IT'S BEEN a few weeks since everything happened and I'm still trying to get myself out of this funk. My parents have been a big help with Reign and when Quran wants to see her he has to go through them. I couldn't stand to look at his face yet. I know sooner or later I will have to but right now I just can't do it. I still keep crying but not as much. Tatiana has still been trying to call me but there is nothing she can say to me for me to even consider being her friend again.

Gabi and Keysha has called me or came by a few times to check on me and help me out with Reign as well. Today was a beautiful day out and I decided today would be the day I would get up off my ass and stop feeling sorry for myself. I was in need of getting groceries, as well as getting my hair done and a manicure and pedicure. So that's exactly what I was going to do.

After getting my hair, nails, and feet done I headed to the grocery store. As I was trying to find the right peaches I saw this fine ass guy walking by with the most gorgeous beard I ever saw in my life. It was nice and full and shiny. I just wanted to pull on it. He was brown skin, tall and kinda stocky. All he had on was a white tee, some jeans and some boots but he made that simple outfit look good as hell. I shouldn't be having thoughts like this so soon after my breakup but he was too damn fine. Next thing I know he's standing right next to me.

"What's ya number ma?" Damn he was fine I said to myself while looking at him up and down.

"Well damn straight to the point, no hello, how are you, what's your name, nothing huh."

He chuckled, "nah I can say all that shit after you give me your number."

"So you just knew i was going to give you my number? A little cocky are we."

"I wouldn't call it cocky but I like to go after things I want and I liked what I saw so I'm going after it" he said smirking at me.

"Well sir what if I told you I wasn't going to give you my number?"

"Then I'll say it's cool but trust me I'll see you again and next time you won't be playing hard to get."

"Hmm, I guess we'll see huh."

"You take care sweetheart," he said as he winked at me and walked away.

As I continued shopping all I could think about was that fine ass dude. Shaking those thoughts out of my head I called up Gabi to see if her and Keysha would like to go out sometime this week for dinner and drinks. Even though we've spoken on the phone, I missed seeing my girls.

"Hey girl, I said to Gabi, what's going on?"

"Nothing much, how are you?"

"I'm feeling pretty good today, I was wondering if you wanted to meet up for dinner and drinks Friday night."

"Yes that's cool, let me up Keysha to see if she wants to come."

"Alright so we'll meet at Applebees since they have some good strawberry margaritas and they are only a dollar this month, let's say around 7, is that cool?"

"Yup that works for me, see you Friday," Gabi said then hung up.

I couldn't wait until Friday I really need to have a few drinks and have a good time. This whole Quran and Tatiana thing was still bothering me but I was slowly getting over it. I mean he was my first love and gave me my little girl so how can I get over him so easily. Shit even with Tati we've been through so much together so it won't be that easy to just forget about her so easy but fuck it life goes on right. Now I do hope I run into the cutie from the grocery because baby was fine. It may be too soon to move on but they say one way to get over one man is to get under another and he is definitely someone I can see myself getting under.

TEN

FRIDAY NIGHT ROLLED AROUND and I was excited to be getting out. We all decided to just meet there so after I finished getting dressed I was headed out. Tonight I had on a black pencil skirt, with a pink tee and a black blazer over it and some wedge heels. Walking up to the table both girls were already there.

"Hey bitches!" I yelled as I hugged and kissed Gabi then Keysha.

"What's up girl, your looking cute."

"Thank you, thank you I try" I laughed.

"So Kam what's going with you?"

"Chile, Quran, and Tatiana keep calling me trying to apologize and shit but there is nothing anyone can say to me to make me accept the shit they did. Of course I had to talk to Quran since we do have a child together. I let him come over a couple of days ago and damn if he wasn't looking and smelling good but bitch I wasn't falling for it. He apologized talking about he didn't want to lose his family, blah, blah, blah. I told his ass you should have thought about that before you stuck your dick in my best friend."

"Right, right" Gabi co-signed.

"Well I say fuck him and fuck her hoe ass too," Keysha said as she high fived Gabi.

"Enough about them two, let me tell y'all about this fine ass dude I saw in the grocery store the other day. He was... and before I got a chance to tell them I heard this deep baritone voice next to me."

"Don't stop your story now ma, he was what, I'm curious to see what you were going to say about me" he smirked raising one eyebrow.

Clearing my throat I said "well there is no need to say it now since your standing right here," I nervously giggled.

"I told you I was going to see you again sweetheart. I told myself that if I saw you again I wasn't gonna let you get away. Jamil is the name by the way he said while grabbing my hand."

"I'm Kamaya and these are my girls Gabi and Keysha" I pointed to the both of them.

"Nice to meet y'all beautiful ladies," he said while still holding my hand. "Well Miss Kamaya I don't want to hold you ladies up any more than I have so here's my number, make sure you use it." He kissed my hand, winked at my girls and walked away.

"Damn, was that the guy from the supermarket that you were about to tell us about?" Keysha asked me.

"That sure is and his ass was cocky as hell in the store but I low key liked it. Like I was trying to tell y'all, he walked up on me all like what's your number ma. He didn't even say hello or nothing he just got straight to the point. So I kindly turned his ass down, and his response was basically when I see you again I'm not letting you get away. Since that day I kept thinking about his sexy ass and I was hoping I saw him again, so best believe I will be calling him but I'm gonna make him sweat a little."

A Couple Weeks Later

It's been a while, I'm not who I was before
You look surprised, your words don't burn me anymore
Been meaning to tell ya, but I guess it's clear to see
Don't be mad, it's just a brand new kinda me
It can't be bad, I found a brand new kinda free

The sun was shining and I was feeling good, and as I was listening to Alicia Keys I thought about finally calling Jamil. Connecting my phone to the Bluetooth I dialed his number and waited for him to answer.

"Yo what's good?" his deep voice came through my speakers.

"Hey Jamil it's Kamaya the girl you met a couple of weeks ago."

"Damn ma I thought I was never gonna hear from you. I was getting ready to stake out at the grocery store to try to catch you again" he chuckled.

"Ha, I was going to call but I had to get my mind right first, I had a few things going on."

"I hear that sweetheart but what's up though, you been thinking about a nigga huh."

"I mean you crossed my mind a time or two" I giggled. He crosses my mind a little more than a time or two but I wasn't going to tell him that. Honestly I haven't stopped thinking about him since the day I first saw him in the store.

"Fa sho, fa sho, I definitely been thinking about your sexy ass too, but what you got going on tonight maybe we can hit up a movie or something. Do you like scary movies?"

"Yeah I do, that movie Insidious just came out, maybe we can check that out," I told him. I loved scary movies, I hope he did too.

"Okay ma that's cool, don't be all scared and shit" he chuckled.

"Nah scary movies don't scare me, your the one that's going to be scared sir."

"Well Ms Lady shoot me your address and I'll come pick you up around 9, the movie starts at 9:30."

"Cool, I'll see you later."

Ever since that movie night we've been spending as much time as we can together. With both of us being busy we agreed on having date night at least once a week. Tonight we are going to a comedy and I'm really looking forward to it. I haven't gotten any clothes lately and since I still have some baby weight I called up Gabi and Keysha to see if they wanted to hit the mall up with me. Grabbing my phone off the dresser I called Keysha first and I was gonna have her call Gabi on three way.

"Keysha what's up girl?"

"I know this isn't Kam calling me" she responded, girl it's like I haven't talked to you in weeks."

"Hush child it has not been that long, it's only been a couple of days."

"Well it sure feels like it but anyway what do I owe the pleasure of this call."

"I was going to ask if you and Gabi wanted to hit up Menlo Park with me, I need to try to find something to wear on my date tonight."

"Ohh you going out with Mr. Sexy Beard?" she asked me.

"Yes I am but call Gabi first and we'll continue this conversation."

"Okay hold on, hello" Gabi said coming onto the line.

"Hey bitch I screamed out, want to hit up the mall with me and Keysha."

"Yeah Gabi come because Ms. Kam got some tea to spill about her new boo."

"Okay we can meet up in 20, is that cool for y'all?" I asked them both.

"Yup they said at the same time, shit y'all just nosy I said to them. I'll see y'all in 20 minutes."

Pulling up at the mall I got my phone out of my bag to see where the girls were but I got a message from Jamil before I got a chance to call them.

Jamil: I hope your having a good day beautiful, I can't wait to see you later.

Me: Yes handsome I am and I hope you are having a good day as well. I'm excited about our date.

Jamil: Fa Sho well I'll let you get back to what your doing and I'll see you later baby.

Me: Okay talk to you later

When I got out the car Gabi and Keysha were standing by my car smiling at me. "Bitch he must have some good dick the way you smiling", Gabi said hi-fiving Keysha.

"Well heffas I wouldn't know because we haven't went that far just yet. I'm trying to take my time with him because I really like him and I don't want a repeat of Quran happening. Like everything with Jamil is so perfect and I'm so afraid that one day it's all gonna come crashing down. He doesn't give me a reason to think that but you just never know. He texts me all day, he pretty much answers whenever I call and if he doesn't he will call me right back so it's nothing to worry about. I mean he works, coaches basketball, and has kids so he can't be available every second I call you know."

"Oh honey don't stress over something that isn't there. Just take your time and enjoy it for whatever it is. You don't want to ruin the relationship before it really gets started."

"Gab's right Kam just enjoy the moment."

"I guess y'all right, I'll just take it for whatever it is." That was my problem, I had a habit of overthinking things so this time I'm just going to go with the flow.

"Of course we are right, now let's finish trying to find you something to wear."

As we were walking I heard a voice say "babe let's go in Foot Locker" and when I heard the person respond I almost completely lost my shit. At first the girls weren't paying attention until I heard Keysha say "bitch I know that's not Tatiana and Quran in here like some happy ass couple."

"Yes the fuck it is and she just don't know how stupid she looks considering he still keeps begging for me to take him back." As they got closer I noticed the size of her stomach, I know this nigga did not get her pregnant. Now this bitch is heading over here and his dumb ass looks like a deer caught in headlights.

"Hey Kam, Gabi, Keysha" this bitch had the nerve to be all chipper.

"Oh hey ho I mean Tati," Keysha petty ass responded.

"Kam I just came over to try and be cordial since our babies will be siblings, maybe we can put our differences aside," she said to me while rubbing her stomach.

"Bitch I'm over you and your loose pussy ass but what you need to do is tell "our" baby daddy to stop calling me trying to get me to take him back. I guess he stayed with you because I didn't want his dog ass anymore."

"Ha you wish he was still calling ya fat ass but I know that's a lie, I keep him satisfied so he doesn't need you." See I knew that putting our differences aside mess was some bullshit. This bitch just trying to be petty.

I stood there just looking at her like this bitch is out of her mind and she's lucky I don't hit pregnant women or else her ass would have been dragged right outside of this damn Foot Locker. "Hey baby daddy" I said to Quran, his dumb ass looked like he didn't know what to say," oh hey Kam."

"So anyway Ho-tiana I don't have time for your shit so get the fuck out of my face before I forget you're pregnant, but trust bitch when you drop that load I'm dropping your ass."

"Babe you just gonna let her talk to me like that?"

"Well you shouldn't have said anything to her Tati," Quran responded. Those two idiots started arguing so we walked off, I still have to get ready for my date.

ELEVEN

AFTER FINALLY FINDING me a cute little red dress and some black booties we went to get something to eat and I headed home to get ready for this date. Sliding on my watch I heard the doorbell ring at exactly 9:00. Opening the door for Jamil I ran my hand over my hair to make sure it was all in place.

"Damn ma you look sexy as hell," he said while running his tongue over his bottom lip.

"Your not looking too bad yourself cutie. You got the beard all shiny and shit," I said while I lightly tugged on it.

"Go head" he chuckled, "you know I had to make sure it looked good for you since you love it so much."

"You know I do, that shit sexy as hell."

"Aight woman let's get out of here before we are late for the movie."

When we got to the car he opened the door for me and while riding we were just having simple conversations and listening to the R&B playing in the background. I noticed his phone ring a couple of times but he ignored it. Once we arrived at the theater he paid for the tickets and while we were walking to the concession stand his phone rang again.

"Baby can you get the snacks while I take this call real quick?" he walked away answering his phone.

I found it a little weird that he kept ignoring the previous calls and he had to walk away to answer but I know sometimes the kids he coaches call him for personal issues so I'm not going to think too much of it. I think I'm just a little insecure because of my previous relationship.

"Sorry about that baby he said while kissing me on my cheek, that was one of my kids on the team he's having some troubles at home."

"It's cool, trust me I understand, I just got us some popcorn and a coke is that cool with you."

"Yeah ma that's cool."

As we were walking towards the theater some chick walked up to us, "hey Jamil" she said smiling extra hard.

"Oh what's good Chanique?" J responded back to her.

"J why haven't you called me?" she asked him while rubbing his chest. This bitch was really acting like I wasn't standing there.

"Um excuse me bitch but you might want to keep your hands to yourself acting like you don't see me standing here with my man."

"Bitch I saw you standing there but I thought you was his sister or something. Since when did you start fucking with fat bitches J?

This bitch had the nerve to laugh like I won't molly whop her ass across this floor. "Hoe I got ya fat bitch.."

"Kam let's go" Jamil said pulling me away from her. "Baby girl don't pay her no mind. Let's go and try to enjoy this movie."

"Okay but your just going to let this bitch stand there rubbing on you but didn't say shit and your are going to tell me what her significance is as soon as we leave this damn movie."

"Babe I did move her hand though and no doubt baby I got you, but she don't mean shit."

During the whole movie his scary ass kept jumping and I laughed the whole time. "Bruh how ya grown ass scared of a damn movie?" I asked laughing so hard I had tears in my eyes.

"Man go head but yo ass gonna be scared when I give you this dick" he said standing so close behind me I could feel his dick on my butt. A bitch started to get nervous, it's been a while since I had sex and the way that thing felt I know it's gonna be a problem.

"Oh no don't get quiet now, you was talking all that shit and laughing at me, now you want to act like you can't talk" he smirked.

"Oh nah I'm good" I tried to reassure myself more than him.

Driving back to my house I wondered if tonight was going to be the night. Pulling up at my house he got out to open my door and walk me to my front door.

"So woman you gonna let me in tonight or what?" He asked coming closer to me.

"First you going to tell me about that bitch at the movie theater."

"Man she just some chick I used to fuck with a little minute ago. I stopped calling her so I guess she all in her feelings and shit. You don't have to worry about her or any other bitches."

"I sure hope I don't because I wouldn't have a problem beating a bitch ass and I'm not about to be playing with you either."

"Ha, okay tough guy, can we go in the house now?"

"Yeah let's go but I meant what I said J."

Once we go inside I went to take my shoes off and turn on some music and as soon as Miguel's Use Me started playing Jamil pushed me up against the wall. *Sedate me, salacious salty and sweet I'm overwhelmed by tasty thoughts of you,* he started singing the shit in my ear.

"Baby Girl I've been dreaming of tasting you since the day we met" he whispered in my ear as he started rubbing my ass. *Sensation as I place my tongue on your lips, your overwhelmed by everything I do,* he kissed me with so much passion I got weak in the knees.

"Baby I'm just getting started" he said as he lifted me up and I wrapped my legs around his waist. While still kissing me he slid my panties to the side and starting playing with my pussy. "Damn baby she wet and ready for me." After about a few minutes he lifted me up even higher and began to lick my swollen clit. He was alternating between licking and sucking on it and I was losing my mind. Before I got a chance to cum he put me back down and carried me to my room still making love to my mouth. Once he laid me on the bed he slowly started caressing my breast and he began licking my left nipple.

"Don't worry I won't neglect the right one" he huskily said. Going back and forth between my nipples was causing me to get chills. He then began to make a trail of kisses down my body until he got to my pussy and began devouring it as if his life depended on it. I felt like he snatched my soul straight from my body. "Don't cum until I tell you to" it was feeling so good I had tears in my eyes. "Please, please" I begged him.

"Please what babygirl, tell me what you need."

"Please can I cum?" "yes baby give it to me" and as soon as he said that I had the biggest orgasm of my life. He came up with his beard covered in my juices and that shit was such a turn on. He looked at me in my eyes so deeply and began kissing me, letting me taste my juices on his tongue then he suddenly slammed his dick in me.

Considering it's been a minute and he is bigger than Quran it hurt for a few minutes but after a few strokes I started to adjust to it and it was feeling hella good. He was making love to my body in a way that I never felt before. With each slow stroke I felt like our souls were combining. For the rest of the night he took me to a whole new level of sexual pleasure and I came so many times I lost count.

TWELVE

I HAVE REALLY BEEN ENJOYING Jamil's company for the last few months and I'm at the point where I feel like I'm in love with him. We even have dates where I take Summer Reign with us and she loves him. Sometimes she acts like she likes him more than me. Everything is just perfect with us, sometimes I feel it's a little too perfect. Like right now I'm sitting here looking at this bouquet of lilies he sent me a few minutes ago. At least once a week he sends me flowers or something with little notes attached with different quotes or sometimes it's little jokes. Today's note says "Since You've Been Around I Smile More Than I Used To." I couldn't help but to sit there and blush because I've been the same way lately. I feel things with him that I didn't feel with Quran. It's like Jamil is my best friend as well as lover. He's definitely more intimate than Quran ever was.

Speaking of Quran he's calling me yet again. "What is it Quran?"

"Damn Kam why you have to be so mean all the time, I'm just trying to talk to my baby momma."

"What do we need to talk about, you moved on and I moved on so what, what is it?"

"Look I'm only with her because you wouldn't take me back and now she's pregnant but if you say the word I'll leave her ass in a hot second and we can take care of the baby together. I need you and my baby girl back in my life full time. I hate coming over to see or get the baby and feel like I am a stranger."

"It's because you are a stranger Quran, because only a stranger would do the shit you did to me and the fact that you would just up and leave your pregnant girlfriend tells me you still ain't shit and there is no way we are getting back together so get the fuck off my phone and I'll see you next week when it's time for you to pick up your daughter." "But Kam.." I hung up on his ass, what the fuck he think this is. First he cheats on me with the bitch, gets her pregnant, starts a whole relationship with her and thinks I would want to be back with him, nah son you got me fucked up.

Not even two seconds later my phone rung again, thinking it was Quran I snapped. "What! What the fuck do you want!"

"Whoa, whoa baby girl who got you all upset?" Oh it was only Jamil. "My bad I thought you were my daughter's father calling me again."

"Fuck that nigga sweetheart don't let him get you all upset, anyway I hope your getting ready for our little getaway this weekend."

"Yes I am because I can definitely use a break from everything and everyone."

"Don't worry baby I got you, I'm gonna take your mind off that fuck nigga and everything else you got going on, it's just gonna be about you all weekend, ya heard."

"Well I can't wait, I'm actually about to start packing my bags now. I like to get myself prepared early."

"Aight ma I'll leave you to it and I'll talk to you later."

"Wait! where are we even going?"

"It's a surprise" he said and hung up. Well since I have no clue where we are going I'll just pack a couple different outfits.

Saturday morning Jamil arrived at my house at 8am on the dot. I was so excited about going somewhere for a whole weekend with him that I barely slept. It was going to be nice spending time alone for a couple of days. I was already on the porch waiting for him.

"Damn ma you couldn't wait to leave huh" he chuckled as he stepped out of the car with some grey sweatpants, a grey T-shirt and some Nike slides on. His outfit was so simple but he still looked so good in it, just looking at him had my juices flowing.

"Yup! I told you I was ready to go. I'm like a little kid when it's time to go somewhere especially surprises."

"I see, I see" he said while grabbing my bags. "You sure packed a lot of stuff to just be gone for two days."

"Well you didn't tell me where we were going so I had to be prepared for any and everything."

"I hear you, well let's go so we can stop and get some breakfast first."

"Soo are you still not going to tell me where we are going?"

"Nope so don't ask me anymore miss lady, just sit back and relax."

After eating we ended up at the airport, so you know my excitement was really kicking in, I started dancing in my seat.

He walked around the car to help me out, "come on crazy girl" he laughed. "You act just like a little kid."

"It's because I'm excited duh, don't make fun of me" I said punching him in his arm.

"Nah baby I think it's cute, I'm happy that I can make you happy."

"Good, good now let's go so we can get to this surprise."

We finally got checked in and we were on our way. I was a little nervous about flying so I decided to take a nap. Waking up a couple hours later I realized we were in Miami.

"Oh my god babe, I can't believe we are in Miami!" I always wanted to come here but never made it.

"Baby this is just the beginning, stick with a nigga like me and I'll show you the world."

A few minutes later we ended up at a hotel not too far from the airport. We checked in and headed up to our room, apparently we had a penthouse suite. It had two bedrooms, two bathrooms and it had its own private balcony. Not sure why we needed so much space but whatever. This shit was nice as hell.

"This room is so nice, I don't think I ever want to leave it."

Chuckling he said "we have to leave sooner or later, we have plans for dinner tonight at the rooftop restaurant."

"Oh okay, well I want to check out the rest of the hotel."

"Woman I'm tired so you go head while I take a little nap."

"Okay babe I'll be back in a little bit," I said kissing his lips. I'm gonna take a quick shower and change real quick before I go. He pulled me back by my shirt, kissing me again. "You sure you want to leave right now?"

"Yes J, I promise I'll be back in a little bit." Okay, okay, he said laying down.

I went downstairs to see what else the hotel had to offer. They had a bar, a spa that I definitely was going to try to check out, and a little souvenir shop. I'm gonna have to come back later, but for now I think I'm gonna head over to the bar and have a little drink while I let J get some sleep. Sitting at the bar I ordered a glass of Pinot Grigio, and I noticed this handsome guy looking at me but I tried to ignore him considering I'm on vacation with my boyfriend and I'm happy so no need to cause any unwanted drama.

After about 10 minutes of him constantly watching me I guess he decided to make his way over to me.

"Hello beautiful, can I get you another drink?" Damn did he have to be that fine.

Now my mind was saying no because I do have a boyfriend who was right upstairs but at the same time what's wrong with a little harmless drink, right. So of course I said, "yes I'll take another one."

He called the bartender over and ordered himself a Hennessy and coke, and he said whatever the young lady is having.

"I'll just take another glass of Pinot Grigio, thank you."

After our drinks came he turned and looked at me and asked, "so what's a pretty lady like you doing in a bar by yourself?"

"I just came down here to have a drink and to relax for a moment that's all. What about you sir?"

"I just came to have a drink myself before I meet up with my brother. I'm Khai by the way, nice meeting you Ms..." "Kamaya, nice to meet you'" I told him while shaking his hand.

We sat there talking for a little bit, he told me he was in Miami on business and I told him I was on a mini vacation with my boyfriend. As we were sitting there just laughing and joking he was suddenly snatched off the bar stool.

"Aye nigga what the fuck you all in my girl face for!" J exclaimed.

Khai held up his hands in surrender, "that was some real sucker shit you just did but I'm gonna let you slide. No need to be fighting in front of this pretty lady but if I catch you in the streets again best believe you gonna see me."

Before things got anymore out of hand I started to push J away from him and as we walked away I looked back and mouthed "I'm sorry" to Khai.

He just smiled and winked at me. I hate that our little encounter ended like that but I'll probably never see him again anyway so it doesn't even matter. He was cute and all but I'm good.

"J what was all that about, why you yoke that dude up like that?"

"Bae I didn't like how he was all in your face and I have to let these niggas know you are mine."

"Well I told him I had a boyfriend, it was just an innocent conversation."

"Ain't shit innocent about these niggas out here, you out here looking all sexy and shit so I know what that nigga was thinking because I was thinking the same thing."

" And what were you thinking?" I asked him with one eyebrow raised.

"Shit girl I was thinking how I can't wait to get you back to the room, I'm ready to skip dinner."

"Boy please you know I'm not skipping dinner," I laughed.

"Yeah I know fatty so let's go, and you gonna get enough of that boy shit too."

THIRTEEN

I REALLY DIDN'T EXPECT for Jamil to act like that from someone just having an innocent conversation with me. He told me that it bothered him seeing another dude in my face and he was a little jealous. I assured him it wasn't nothing because it really wasn't, even though the dude was fine as hell. Anyway I'm not going to dwell on it too much, I just hope he's not going to let it ruin our date tonight or the rest of the trip for that matter.

"Kam, Kam," I heard him calling me, "huh you called me?" I must have really zoned out for a minute.

"Yeah crazy girl, you must have been having some serious thoughts over there. I was asking you if you had any idea of what you want to eat."

"No I haven't looked at the menu yet. Looking over the menu I saw they have a ravioli dish but it had truffles on it."Um since when do they put chocolate in food?" I was really confused by that.

"What are you talking about woman?" He looked at me like I was crazy.

"This says ravioli with truffles, and the only truffles I know is chocolate so I'm not going to eat chocolate on ravioli."

Laughing at me he said, "truffles are a type of mushroom crazy not just chocolate."

"Oh well if that's the case I'll have the ravioli with the truffles. How did you even know that?"

"The food network, you know a nigga like me likes to eat so I be trying to learn new shit to cook."

"Well when are you going to cook for me sir?"

"Soon baby real soon. I'll come over to your place and make you a nice meal."

After he said that it got me to thinking, we never go to his house and I'm wondering why. "J, how come we never go to your house?"

"Huh, oh um because you know I have roommates and shit and I don't want them niggas all in your face and I know they will be."

"Babe ain't nobody thinking about me," I told him. Apart of me felt like he could have been lying but I really didn't have a reason to think that so I guess I'll" just go with what he said for now.

"Girl you fine as fuck and thick as hell so I know they would be all over ya ass and I'm not trying to fight with my boys."

"If you say so" I said to him rolling my eyes.

"On some real shit tho Kam I'm falling in love with ya sexy chocolate ass."

"Wow J I didn't know you felt that way but to be honest with you I'm falling in love with you as well."

"Oh shit girl you got a nigga over here blushing, well let's hurry up and finish this dinner so we can go back to the room and I can really show you how I feel."

"I thought we were going to do something else after this, like sightsee and just walk around, it's a beautiful night so we should be out enjoying it. Trust me it would be worth the wait."

"Well shit girl since you put it that way I guess we can go for a walk and see what the Miami night life is about."

"Good because I saw a little club I think we should check out down the street."

"So you want me to go to a club with you and let even more niggas see ya fine ass, nah you trying to make me catch a case out here."

I started cracking up and he looked at me all serious like he wasn't playing. "Boy ain't nobody catching no cases, let's go and have some fun, I'm trying to get the full Miami experience."

After we walked down the street for a few minutes we ended up at the club and it was packed. I'm praying that some more shit don't pop off. As soon as we got inside that thought went out the window because sure enough of I saw Khai with his boys and I was hoping J didn't see him. Welp I lost hope pretty quick because two seconds later Jamil spotted him too.

"There go ya boy" he said to me.

"That is not my boy J don't start." I wasn't trying to go there with him.

"I'm coolin baby as long as he don't bring his ass over here we straight. Okay let's go get some drinks."

After getting our drinks and making our way to the dance floor everything was going good until suddenly I see Khai headed towards our direction, please don't let him come over here. Oh shit here we go I thought the closer he got to us.

"What's good Miss Kamaya?" he said winking at me. Since I'm not rude, well shit sometimes I am, but not today so I spoke back.

"Hi Khai," now why did I do that. My ass should have pretended like I didn't even see him.

"Oh you just a disrespectful ass nigga huh?" Jamil said. Oh boy here we go, please don't let these fools start fighting in here.

"Nah bruh I'm not, but it ain't nothing wrong with me speaking to the young lady."

"Actually bruh yes the fuck it is disrespectful, you see me and my girl just trying to have a good time and you want to come over here with that pussy shit."

"My nigga I'm far from pussy and you only got away with that shit earlier because you caught me off guard but what's up now!"

Next thing I know these two fools are fighting in the middle of the club. Security and Khai's boys were trying to break it up but at first they were having a hard time doing so, finally after a few minutes they got them both to separate.

Khai was yelling out "I told ya punk ass I'm far from a pussy"! I started to push J away from him so we can get out of here.

"I'm sorry baby I didn't mean for all that to happen and I'm gonna make it up to you, let's stop and get some champagne on the way back to the room."

"Ok J, that's fine with me." I was a little pissed though because there was no need for him to act like that. We finally made it back to our room about twenty minutes later and I decided to take a shower and put on this nice little lingerie outfit I got just for J and tonight I'm going to do a little dance for him. Stepping out of the bathroom with a deep red one piece outfit with a plunging neckline, it made my breasts sit up nice and perky and my fat ass look even fatter. I put on Dance for you by Beyoncé. *I just wanna show you how much I appreciate you,* I walked over to him and pushed him down in the chair. *Wanna show you how much I'm dedicated to you,* I slowly rocked my hips back and forth, *Wanna show you how much I will forever be true,* I dropped down low and began rubbing my hands all over him then I got back up and walked away from him, *wanna show you how much I value what you say,* then I slowly crawled over to him, then he suddenly grabbed me and placed me on his lap, *I wanna show you how much I really care about your heart,* I started slow grinding on his lap.

"Damn girl I can't take no more of this, you looking sexy ass fuck right now and you got my dick hard as hell."

I got up and walked to the bedroom and made sure I put an extra switch in my walk. "Make sure you grab that champagne," I told him.

"Don't worry I got it," he came jogging after me.

As soon as we made it to the room he pushed me back on the bed then he started taking his clothes off. I couldn't help to bite my lower lip, his ass is so fucking sexy, he's definitely been working out. He popped open the champagne and began pouring all over me and licked it off each place he poured it, starting from my neck, to my breasts, my stomach, and when he poured it on my pussy he began slurping it off so I lost my damn mind.

"Mhmm baby that feels so good." I never felt sensations like this before. He had me ready to propose to his ass.

"You gonna cum for daddy, ma?"

"Yes daddy, I'm cummin, I'm cummin!" I screamed out. It felt like I was never gonna stop cummin, I was ready to roll over and put my thumb in my mouth.

"Don't tap out on me now babygirl, you taking all this dick tonight" and I did just that. He made love to my entire body for the rest of the night.

FOURTEEN

WHEN I WOKE up Jamil wasn't in the bed but I heard him in the bathroom whispering on the phone. I wonder why he's whispering, maybe so he doesn't wake me up. My nosey ass couldn't hear what he was saying so I just laid there thinking about last night. It was definitely one of the best nights of my life, well minus the fight.

That Khai dude was fine as hell and obviously wasn't no sucker. If I was single I most certainly would have liked to talk to him some more. We just had this chill ass vibe but J was my baby and I wasn't going to mess that up for nobody. After a few more minutes J came out of the bathroom.

"Good morning beautiful I didn't realize you were up." He walked over and kissed me.

"Good morning to you too handsome and I've only been up for a couple of minutes, I thought you left without me."

"Nah I just had to handle my hygiene and I ordered us some breakfast, room service should be bringing it up any minute now." Maybe that's who he was on the phone with and I'm over here about to start tripping about nothing.

Knock, knock, room service, he went to go get the food so I decided to get up and handle my hygiene as well. When I walked back to front room I noticed a shit load of food.

"Damn baby I know I'm a big girl but this is a lot of food, whose supposed to eat all of this?"

"Baby ain't nothing wrong with your size but I ordered all of this so we can have a variety, I wasn't sure exactly what you wanted so I got everything you can think of. Come have a seat and eat with your man."

We had everything fruits, eggs, bacon, sausages, waffles, and pancakes. As well as orange and apple juice, milk, and some champagne.

"What would you like to eat sweetheart?" he asked getting up to fix my plate.

"I'll just have some fruit first then just a little eggs and some waffles."

"No problem baby and I'm gonna make us some mimosas."

"Uh don't you think you had enough champagne last night mister?"

"Ha yeah but I can use a little more and I might just save some for later on," he said winking at me.

He sat down next to me and began feeding me some strawberries with whipped cream.

"Hmm, baby these strawberries are so good."

Yeah I see, you have the juice dripping down the side of your mouth, let me get that for you" he said licking the side of my mouth. Girl you keep it up and we going to be using that whipped cream for something else.

"I got a couple of things I can do with it but I would like to eat first."

"Shit I want to eat too but not this food," suddenly he was on the floor eating my pussy while I was trying to eat my waffles.

Mmmmm, I damn near choked on my food. Oh daddy that feels so good, I'm about to cum.

"Give it all to me baby," and just like that I came and he didn't waste a drop. Mhmm, mhmm he said coming back up licking his lips, now I can eat some real food. I just sat there unable to move, his ass had me weak. "Eat up woman because we have things to do today."

Whew I need a second to get my breathing under control. A couple of seconds later we both continued to eat and have regular conversation.

"Babe I just want to say thank you for bringing me here, I'm enjoying myself and a girl can get used to this. Everything is perfect, well maybe not that fight last night," I said to him laughing.

"Shit girl that nigga was asking for it, he was willing to fight over you and he don't even know you."

"No J he wanted to fight you because of what happened at the hotel earlier."

"I couldn't control myself baby, I saw him all in your face and lost it. I'll do that shit again too if I have to, you mines and I'm not afraid to let these niggas know."

"Okay tough guy you don't have to worry about nobody else I'm all yours baby."

"Woman I know that, now come over and give me a kiss." Getting up, I made why way over to him and straddled his lap and began kissing all over his face. "Alright now don't start nothing you can't finish."

"Oh baby I can start it and most definitely finish it."

"Girl you talking big shit right now, you lucky we have to get out of here or I'll have you calling me GOD again."

"Boy please I was not calling you GOD," I said getting up from his lap.

"Shit it sounded like it to me he said slapping me on my ass."

"Sure, I'm going to take a shower and get ready. While I was in the shower I heard the door open, J don't come in here because I know you and we would never get out of here."

"What girl, I'm just trying to kill time by getting in with you." Mmhmm, and next thing I know he's kissing all on my neck.

"See J I told you, I knew you was going to start some shit."

"I'm not starting anything but I couldn't help to kiss you, your like a chocolatey Hershey's kiss."

"Whatever, can you wash my back for me?" He began washing me all over and I in turn washed him all over. As I rubbed the wash-cloth over his dick it started to get hard and it was looking so yummy that I had to suck it.

Dropping down on my knees he said "Kam what you doing?" "Oh nothing I just want to show you how much I appreciate what you do for me," Then I slowly kissed the head of his dick.

"Don't tease me girl suck that shit like you mean it" he said grab-bing my hair. Once he did that I deep throated his dick until I felt it at the back of my throat. The first couple of times I gagged but once I relaxed my throat I sucked on it like my life depended on it.

"Damn girl that shit feels so good, just like that." He had a tight grip on my hair but I loved that shit. I started to suck on his balls and I thought he was going to snatch my hair out of my head. He started pumping harder and he shot his load down my throat. "Damn ma, that shit was good, that's why I love yo ass."

"I love you too baby now let's get out of here so we can go." A couple minutes later we got out the shower and continued to get ready for our day. I kept my outfit simple since we were going to be walking around all day. I just put on a cute pair of skinny jeans and a pink T-shirt and some pink Chuck Taylor's. Only jewelry I put on was some little pink ball earrings and my pink baby G Shock watch. J was dressed simple as well with some jeans, a t-shirt, some black Chucks, and his black G shock. Both of our outfits were simple but we both still looked fly.

We decided to walk the strip that we were staying on. They had a few stores so we went to get some new clothes and sneakers and he got a couple of things for his kids and I got a couple of things for my baby girl. He even bought me a new Coach wallet and pocketbook. Coming out of the Coach store we saw a familiar face.

"Oh look its your little friend Chanique this bitch better not come over here with her shit." Why did I think she would just keep on walking, messy bitches like her always have to make a scene.

"Hey Jamil, I see your still fucking with miss piggy." This bitch was really testing my patience.

"Bitch I told you the last time I saw you.." "hold up baby," J said holding me back.

"Listen here Chanique what me and you had is and was over a minute ago, stop calling me and don't ever come for my girl again or the next time I'm letting her whoop yo ass." When he let me go I got real close to her face, "bitch that one right there is off limits, I said pointing at J, so I suggest you move the fuck on."

"It's cool hoe, wait until you find out the real truth about him."

"Yeah whatever bitch just the move the fuck on."

When we walked away I asked him exactly what did she mean when I find out the real truth, what was that about. "Nothing ma she's just trying to say stuff to fuck with you. Don't let her or nobody else fuck up the rest of our trip. Remember it's just you and me baby, I love you girl."

"I love you too," and with that being said we went on to enjoy the rest of our little getaway.

FIFTEEN

IT'S BEEN a few days since we came back and I haven't heard from Jamil since he dropped me off after our trip. I hope everything is okay with him, I know more than likely he's just been busy with his kids and work. I tried calling him but he didn't answer the phone, sometimes he doesn't answer right away but he usually calls me right back. Gabi and Keysha were on their way over so I got up to clean up a little and make us something to eat. I had a taste for some spaghetti and garlic bread so that's what we were having and I had a bottle of wine that I brought back from Miami so I figured why not pop it open. Once I put the water on for the noodles I heard the doorbell ring so I went to let them in.

"Hey y'all" I said to both of them giving them both a hug and kiss on the cheek.

"Hey girl look at you looking all extra chocolate and shit. Miami must have been good to you."

"Girl was it but it was some other shit that happened that could have ruined it but we didn't let it."

"Well shit fill us in, Gabi said. Wait do we need a drink for this?"

"Honey we most certainly do, I told them getting up to get the bottle of wine."

"This shit must be extra juicy if you had to get a whole bottle" laughed Keysha.

"Let me start by saying Miami is amazing, we definitely have to plan a girls trip there some time soon."

"All you have to do is tell me when," they both said.

"So anyway, J told me that he was falling in love with me and I told him I was falling in love with him as well and after that he made love to my entire body, I felt things that I never felt before. Chile he even poured champagne all over me and licked it off. Let's just say everytime I see a bottle of champagne I will be having flashbacks, I said laughing. I even did a little dance for him y'all and you know I be all shy about shit like that but he loved it."

"Embrace it girl, shit if he likes you better love it."

"Oh and why that girl Chanique was down there like she was stalking him or something, I was ready to dig in her ass again but he stopped me this time and told her that they were done and to stop calling him and the next time she wouldn't be saved from an ass whooping. She did say something that kind of bothered me though but I kept my cool. She mentioned something about I'll find out the real truth about Jamil, I don't even know what that's supposed to mean."

"Well what did he say in response to that?" asked Keysha.

"All he said was don't worry about what she was saying because she was just trying to say stuff to get me upset. I'm not going to lie it did work a little because sometimes he seems a little distant, he doesn't always answer when I call and even the other morning when we were in Miami I heard him in the bathroom whispering on the phone. Now I know he called room service so maybe that was it or he was checking on his kids and didn't want to wake me up. I haven't talked to him since we got back the other day and when I called earlier he didn't answer and he still hasn't called me back and it's been hours."

"Honey don't stress yourself, he's probably just trying to get things back on track with work and the kids since y'all were gone for a couple of days."

"I guess you're right. Besides he can't be doing too much since we were able to go out of town for a few days and up until now we talked everyday and seen each other just as much so I'm gonna stop tripping before I make something out of nothing."

"Yeah her hoe ass is just jealous he cut her off and she don't want you with him, that's all" said Gabi.

"Fuck her and I guess the truth will come to the light sooner or later, but let me finish telling y'all about the rest of the trip. So when we get there we are in this penthouse suite, I mean the room was everything. Anyway he was tired and of course I wanted to look around so after I showered and changed I went to check out the rest of the hotel. They had spa, which I had to go to, a bar and some other little stuff. I went to the bar to get a little drink you know loosen up a little and this fine ass dude just kept looking at me.

Now I'm trying not to pay him any attention I mean I am on vacation with a whole man, a fine one at that but I couldn't deny this guys fineness either. He was tall, brown skin, he had brown bedroom eyes and I just wanted to suck on his bottom lip. Did I mention he has a beard and y'all know I'm a sucka for beards. It wasn't as thick and full like J's, he had a nice close and clean shaven one. Hmm, I felt like being a hoe for a minute but I quickly changed my mind. Anyway, after a few minutes of him staring at me he comes over to buy me a drink and sits right next to me and introduces himself. His name is Khai and I can't lie I felt this connection to him but there's nothing I can do about it because, well you know. So we're talking about any and everything, he tells me he was in Miami for a work conference but I don't know if he was originally from Florida or somewhere else. At that point it didn't even matter, we just had this chill ass vibe and was chilling until J came."

"Oh shit did that nigga spazz out or what?"

"Did he! He snatched his ass off the damn bar stool. The dude Khai played it cool though, he was like no need to be fighting in front of the pretty lady or some shit like that, I don't remember but the shit threw me off. I didn't expect Jamil to react like that, I wasn't doing anything wrong, just having an innocent drink and conversation. But wait that's not all, later on after we had dinner we went to this club that was down the street and guess who was there."

"Who that bitch Chanique?"

"Nope, Khai's ass and this time he wasn't having that let's not fight shit, these two grown ass men started fighting right in the middle of the club. It took security and Khai's boys to finally get them to stop fighting, it was so crazy. After all that we still managed to enjoy the rest of the trip. I'm going to be honest though if I wasn't with J I would have definitely tried to see what was up with Khai."

"Did y'all at least exchange numbers or anything?"

"No, shit after him and J got into it I had to get out of there before it got worse. I did apologize to him though when J had his back turned and you know this nigga had the nerve to wink his damn eye at me. I was thinking he may be just as crazy as Jamil's ass, I laughed. Oh well I'll probably never know."

"Don't say never, hell you never know if you'll see him again or not. If he lives in Miami maybe you'll see him when we go down there."

"It don't matter if I see him again since I am in a relationship. A pretty happy one at that."

"Well girl it is nothing wrong with having friends. These niggas be fucking up so much so it's always good to keep one in the back pocket."

"I'm good, anyway what's going with y'all?"

"Nothing much, I saw Quran and Tatiana though and apparently they are having a girl," said Keysha.

"Oh that's nice, I don't really speak to either one of them unless it concerns my child. I don't wish no harm on them and I hope they have a healthy baby but I can care less about both of their trifling asses."

For the next couple of hours we just sat that there drinking and enjoying our girl time together. These two have been there for me through everything and I don't know where I would be without them. I barely even thought about Jamil all this time and why he hasn't called me.

Suddenly I hear my phone ring, thinking it's him I hurried up and answered and I heard some news that I couldn't even imagine and that would change the course of my relationship with Jamil and hell probably any other relationship in the future. "Hello" I answered.

"Hello who is this?" It was some chick asking me who is this and her ass the one that called me.

"Um who is this you called me!" I was about to get pissed, I hate when people do that dumb shit.

"Well I'm calling because your number keeps coming up in my husband's phone." Wait a minute did she just say her husband, I know this nigga wasn't married all this damn time.

"Excuse me did you say husband?" I hope I heard her wrong but I know I probably didn't. Now everything was starting to make more sense. The not answering when I call, the couple of times he would walk away to answer the phone, the whispering, all that shit. It's crazy how you overlook the signs that are right in your face.

"Yes Jamil is my husband and we have been married for the last four years." I couldn't even respond to her as the tears fell from my eyes and my phone went crashing down to the floor. Once again I got played like a fool.

SIXTEEN

"KAMAYA, KAM!" I keep hearing the girls calling me but i couldn't respond to either one of them. I just continued to stand there with tears falling from my eyes. How can he have a whole wife and not tell me? How can he tell me he loves me but hurt me the way I feel right now? What would make him to lead me on like this? I have so many questions but I don't even know where to begin, hell I can't even move out of this spot I'm in.

"Kamaya honey you're scaring us, what happened? Who was on the phone?" Gabi asked me.

"He..he's married" I cried out.

"Who's married? Don't tell me Quran married hoe ass Tatiana!" Keysha expressed.

"No, Jamil is married, apparently he had a wife for the last four years and that's who that was that just called me."

"Wait so you're telling me that he has a whole fucking wife even though yall spend so much time together. Like this nigga just took you on a vacation, he's fighting niggas and shit but he has a wife."

"Yes Gab, that's exactly what I'm saying. A whole fucking wife that he never once mentioned to me. I never saw him wear a ring or any type of indication that there was anyone else. With the exception of the one time i heard him whispering and today he never answered my calls or text messages but other than that i had no idea that he could have been married. I feel like a fool all over again. I thought he was different. How could he do me like this after i told him what i went through with Quran. His words were always don't worry Kam, it's just me and you and of course I believed him, i said as i started crying again. I actually thought that maybe we would eventually get married, but I guess not unless he's into polygamy, I'm sure the fuck not. I was even considered having another baby with him."

"Maybe they are separated Kam, don't jump the gun unless you get all the facts from him," Keysha said trying to be the voice of reason.

"Fuck that! That bitch wouldn't have felt so comfortable to call if she they were separated and not really still together. Kamaya I hate to say it sweetie but I think he is still fully married to her and he's an asshole."

"Gabrielle you could very well be right but like Keysha said maybe I need to get all the facts first. Let me try calling him again to see if he answers."

Well of course he didn't answer. More than likely he's probably home trying to save his marriage and totally forgetting my ass. I just feel so damn stupid like how can I get played yet again. Is there a memo going around saying fuck with Kamaya she's a dummy so it's easy to play her. I couldn't do anything but cry and at this point I just want to be alone.

"Hey guys I think I want to be alone for a little while."

"Aww Kam honey are you sure? We can stay here as long as you want us to."

"No I'll be okay, I'm just going to make some tea and lay down. My head is pounding and I think I should probably take a nap."

"Okay mama, please call us if you need anything," Gabi said while her and Keysha hugged me at the same time. "You know you don't have to go through this alone right?"

"Really I'll be fine. I promise I will call both of yall after I get some rest, I said while walking them to the door." The minute I closed and locked the door I slid down on the floor and just started crying my eyes out. I began questioning everything. What did I do to deserve this? Why would he even try to talk to me knowing he had a wife? Was I just a fuck to him and did he really mean it when he told me he loved me.

I think I laid on the floor right by the front door for hours, or at least that's what it felt like. I finally decided to get up and make me some tea and headed to my bed. I just need to lay down for a little longer. Going into my room I put on some music. As 10 seconds by Jazmine Sullivan played through my speakers I laid there and thought about everything I went through. Not just with Jamil but with Quran as well. I just tried to be a good girl and I get played like I'm some sort of sucker. I started wondering if I would ever find true love. Shit maybe it's not meant for me to be happy. Once the song when off I put it back on it again. Jazmine was saying everything I was feeling at the moment.

You broke my heart with all your lies.

You really should look for an exit cause you running out of time
You know that I can get crazy
When I go off, ain't nobody to tame me.

I can't see us moving past this. I'm not trying to be a side chick to nobody but what do you do when you truly love someone. Shit for all I know he may not want to be with me anymore anyway since his wife found out what's been going on. He has to know that I know by now but he still hasn't called me. My head was pounding, my eyes were red and heavy so I finally let sleep overcome me.

I woke up to this loud ass banging on my door. I knew it couldn't be Gabi or Keysha because they both had a key. Looking at the clock I noticed it was 1 o'clock in the morning. Who the fuck could possibly be at my door this time of night. I seriously hope it isn't J because I'm not sure I can face him right now. Maybe if i ignored it the person would go away. After five minutes the banging continued so I decided to see who it was but best believe I was bringing my gun with me because if it's someone on some fuck shit I will shoot their ass.

Throwing on some clothes I made my way to the door. "Who the fuck is it?" I had to put on the tough voice incase it was a stranger or some shit.

"Kamaya, baby it's me can you open the door?" I know the fuck this nigga ain't decide to come to my house after ignoring me for hours.

"Jamil I don't have shit to say to you right now" I hollered through the door.

"Come on ma please open the door, just hear me out. Let me explain everything to you and the if you want me to I will leave you alone."

"How about NO! I'm not opening shit, you lied to me and then you ignored me all fucking day so right now there isn't shit you can say to me that's worth listening. I suggest you take your lying ass home to YOUR WIFE!"

"Babe I'm not leaving until you open the door and let me talk to you."

"Nah bruh, I suggest you get the fuck away from my door unless you plan on sleeping on the porch. I'm taking my ass back to bed. Peace out buddy."

So for the last few days Jamil has been calling me, popping up at my house, sending flowers, cards, fruit baskets, shit you name it and more than likely he sent it. Hell he even sent me some sneakers. Best believe I wore those shits to but that still isn't going to make up for the lies. Gabi and Keysha told me I should at least hear him out and maybe I will but now is not the time. I was dreading going to the grocery store because I had a feeling Jamil would end up popping up there and sure the fuck as the sky was blue I see his ass strolling towards me as i was looking for some ice cream. Damn he sure was looking good. Not today satan, I refuse to look at him like that.

"Damn Kam so this what I have to do to get a few minutes of your time. I know I fucked up but you got a nigga stalking you in the grocery store."

"No Jamil you got yourself stalking me, all you had to do was give me some time and sooner or later I would have called. Maybe."

"Time, you want time Kam, I can't give you that shit ma, I need you to at least listen to me. A nigga out here stressing without you."

"You stressing without me, tuh, how does your wife feel about that. As a matter of fact imagine how much stress I'm in after finding out that the nigga that I was in love with not only lied to you but was hiding a whole fucking wife. IMAGINE THAT STRESS J!"

"Okay, okay sweetheart I know your stressing just as much as me if not more but we can't have this conversation in the middle of the ice cream section. Let me come by later or you can even meet me somewhere so we can talk. After that if you want we can go our separate ways and never talk again if that's what you desire. But I'm going to be real with you Kam, a nigga ain't gonna let you go that easy, wife or not. So you just let me know when your ready to talk." And with that he left me standing there right in the middle of the ice cream aisle.

SEVENTEEN

FOR WEEKS J was still sending me flowers, fruit baskets and all this other shit. This nigga even sent me a guinea pig. Like who the fuck sends a guinea pig as a forgiveness gift. It was cute though. I named it Peppa like peppa pig who's petty as hell. Anyway let me get back on track here. So after all the shit he sent me I finally decided to hear him out. I'm curious to know what made him withhold that important piece of information and what the hell does he plan on doing now that the cat is out of the bag. Now the question is should I let him come over here or just meet him somewhere. I'm afraid he may come here and my panties may just slide off by themselves. It's been a minute and J knows how to get me every time. Yeah I think we should meet at Starbucks or something. Before I got a chance to call him there was a knock at my door and there was a delivery guy with another damn thing of flowers and this one has a note attached.

"To my Kam, listen ma a nigga out here sick without you. I even cried thug tears the other night while I was laying right next to my wife. Baby you got my mind gone and I can't imagine another nigga snatching you up. I know it's fucked up that I didn't tell you I had a wife and I shouldn't even have approached you but I just couldn't help myself. It was just something about you and I had to have you. When I told you I loved you Kam I really meant that shit. I know shit is fucked up now but I can't let you go Kam. You make me feel things I have never felt before and you make me want to be a better man. Kamaya please don't give up on a nigga, I need you ma. Love Jamil." I don't know what he thought this letter was going to do but right now it's not moving me. He really could have told me the truth from the beginning. We definitely need to talk so let me call his ass right now.

"Hey J."

"Hey, hey Kam, I can't believe you finally called me." Damn why did he have to sound so sexy.

"Yeah well I figured I'd give you a chance to explain yourself. Do you think we can meet up at Starbucks sometime today. Not sure if your free now but I will be in about 15 minutes."

"Fa sho 15 minutes is cool with me. I'll see you there and thank you Kamaya for at least taking the time to meet up."

I decided to make his ass wait so I showed up to Starbucks 30 minutes later instead of 15 and I sat in my car for an extra five minutes. I had to make sure I was on point. I put on these high waisted jeans that accentuated my ass and a crop top. Just because I was a big girl didn't mean I couldn't wear crop tops. Anyway I had to make sure I was extra cute, let this nigga see what he's been missing.

"Damn ma, I thought you weren't coming. You look good," he said to me getting up so he can pull out my chair.

Wait did this nigga get cuter in the last couple of weeks and he got his beard looking extra glossy today. Shit let me get my thoughts back on track. This is not that type of party, at least not today anyway. "Hey Jamil, I thought you would have left by now." I kind of didn't even want to face him.

"Nah baby what I have to say is important so I would have waited all day if I had to."

"Well I'm listening so talk." I really could care less about what he had to say but I figured why not just hear him out.

"Kam listen I didn't mean for any of this to happen the way it did and I didn't mean for you to find out I was married like that. There were so many times I wanted to tell you but I just didn't know how."

"Let me stop you there J, you could have told me that day in the supermarket as a matter of fact you didn't even have to come over and say anything to me at all. You could have told me at the movies, or when we were bowling, hell even in Miami. There were countless amount of times you could have told me but you chose not to. It makes me wonder if any of the shit you ever said to me was real, like do you even really love me?" At this point I was in tears, I thought I did all the crying I could do but I guess now that we were talking about it I was reliving that hurt. "How did you even manage to carry on a whole relationship with me like I was the only one?"

"I'm just gonna lay it all out on the table now Kam."

"Tuh now you are," I scoffed.

"Kam just let me talk okay and when I'm done you can say anything you want to me."

"Go head J." I was getting tired of listening to his sorry's and excuses about why he didn't tell me about his wife.

"So listen yes I'm married and yes I have been for the last four years. Do I love my wife, yes I do but I'm not in love with her anymore. We've been having some issues, our schedules are so different so we barely even spend time together anymore. Do I go around cheating on her? No, but when I saw you in the store that day there was just something about you that pulled me towards you and I couldn't let you get away. You just don't understand how much you mean to a nigga. I'm not going to sit here and bash her because that's not necessary but things with you are different. I feel like you understand me more than she does. You don't judge me and I feel like I can be more of myself with you. With her sometimes I feel like she wants me to be something I'm not and doesn't even want to be. I'm gonna keep it real though I can't sit here and honestly say I'm gonna leave her right now because it's complicated. My kids are involved and I know for a fact I don't want to leave them. At the same time though I don't want to lose you either Kamaya. When I told you I loved you I really meant that shit ma. You truly make a nigga happy on some real shit. I can't guarantee what's going to happen but I really want you to stick with me baby and let's see how this all plays out."

"Thats a lot to think about Jamil, I'm going to need more time to process all of this. So you want me to play second to your wife. It was one thing doing it unwillingly but to know that's what I'm doing doesn't sit well with me. I don't want to be the cause of any more drama you guys may already have."

"Kam baby you can never play second to anybody. I haven't treated you like you were second and there is no way I'm going to start now. I'm always here when you call and we spend a lot of time together and none of that is going to change. A nigga won't be the same without you Kam. I know it's not your ideal relationship but I think we can make this work."

"J I hear all that but no matter how you spin it I will always be second to your wife. Yeah you spend time with me and all that but at the end of the day she comes first. Y'all are legally binded and she is the mother of your children. I just feel like if we continue I will eventually end up being hurt all over again. Hell I'm not completely over you lying to me about all this. I really don't know how to stay with you knowing you are cheating on your wife. Just give me time Jamil please that's all I ask of you."

"I hear you baby and I will give you time but please don't make me wait forever." I'll call you in a few days ma, and then he got up and kissed me on my forehead and left me sitting there in my thoughts.

I watched him walking away and I had to bite my bottom lip. This nigga looked sexy as hell even from the back. Can I really see myself staying with him through all this? Would he even leave his wife for me or hell leave her at all? Not that I want him to leave her for me but where do I fit in at in his life? What happens if he wakes up one day and realizes he doesn't want me anymore? There are so many questions that he wouldn't be able to answer. I'm so afraid to take that chance but at the same time I love him so much. Up until this point he's been perfect, am I really ready to give all that up? I need a drink after all this shit because this little frappuccino ain't cutting it right now.

Instead of getting a drink I ended up going to get Summer Reign and I took her to Chuck E Cheese. This whole situation with Jamil got me feeling upset but I knew spending time with my baby will cheer me up. Unfortunately my good mood didn't last too long because guess who comes waltzing in with his family, yup Jamil with his wife and kids. I just pretended I didn't see him and continued to play with my baby. Every so often when they were close enough to us I would catch him looking at me but I just went on about my business. I'll deal with it another day, right now it's Summer's day so I'm going to make the best of it.

EIGHTEEN

SO I KNOW y'all are probably wondering what I decided to do about Jamil. Well I decided to stick things out with him and see what happens. Is it one of my best choices? Hell no it isn't but I'm in love with him and he always treated me like the queen that I am. I haven't told the girls about my decision, hell I didn't even tell Jamil yet that I want to stick it out with him. As a matter of fact let me call Gabi and Keysha and talk to them about my decision. They probably will try to talk me out of it but I'm going to do what I want regardless but it's nice to get their opinions on it.

"Hey Kesh, hold on while I call Gabi, I need to talk to both of y'all about something."

"So let me give y'all the short version of the conversation that J and I had, he basically told me that yes he still does love his wife but they were having problems. He didn't set out to cheat on her but it was something about me that he couldn't turn away from, so he gave it a shot. Anyways he wants me to still stick it out with him and see how things go and I decided that's what I'm going to do. I'm so nervous about it because he's staying with his wife and who knows if he will ever leave her. I have a strong feeling I will end up getting hurt again but my heart says take a chance." So what do y'all think?

"Well...," Keysha spoke first. "I don't think you should still deal with him but I am going to support you no matter what, but please be careful honey."

"I agree with Keysha to a degree but fuck that nigga Kam! He ain't shit for lying about his wife and he's even worse for suggesting you play second to her. Does he love you? Probably so but at the same time if he really did he would let you go and find real happiness with someone else."

"Trust me I hear what both of y'all are saying but I don't know if it's going to be that easy to give him up you know." Like I love this man wholeheartedly and I'm afraid if I don't take the chance I'll never find love like this again."

"Girl don't think like that, you are a beautiful person inside and out and trust me you will find someone who will love you and only you completely."

"Y'all are right and I appreciate both of y'all being there for me no matter what. I love both of y'all and I don't know where I would be without you two."

"Aww baby we love you too and we will always be here."

I got up to take a nice relaxing bath and I sent J a text message to see if he could come over.

Me: Hey J do you think you can come by?

Jamil: Sure babygirl give me like a hour and I will be there, I'm just finishing up practice.

Me: Okay cool I'll see you in a hour

Now it's been a while since we had sex so no matter what I was getting some from J before he left my house. I made sure I was smelling good, I used my cocoa butter body scrub and my favorite Warm Vanilla Sugar body lotion from Bath and Body Works. I put on one of my lingerie outfits and put my hair up in a bun since he likes it like that and I patiently waited for him to come. For some reason the closer it got for the time for him to come I got nervous. Not sure why I was nervous it's not like it's the first time or something. Maybe because no matter what, the dynamics of our relationship changed. After double checking to make sure everything looked good, I heard the doorbell ring. My heart damn near was beating out of my chest as I walked to the door.

.   .   .

When I opened the door this nigga was looking good as hell and we both just kind of stood there staring at each other like we never saw each other before. Clearing my throat I moved out of the way so he could come into the house.

"Hey Jamil, how are you?" Damn he was looking and smelling extra good today. I hope we can talk first before I end up sliding on his dick. It's been way too long.

"What's good ma?" he replied while licking his lips. "You looking good baby."

Before I even had the door closed he had me pushed up against the wall. "Damn girl I missed the fuck out of you," he said while grabbing me around my neck. He knew I liked it a little rough, he applied just the right amount of pressure. He started using his other hand to rub all over my body then he stuck his fingers in my panties and began rubbing on my clit. Since it's been so long I was on the verge of cumming already when he abruptly stopped and picked me up and carried me to the couch and he put me on all fours and began eating my pussy from the back.

"Hmm girl this pussy taste so good. I missed her baby, did she miss me?"

"Mmm yes baby she missed you," I moaned out while arching my back.

· · ·

"Well show a nigga then," and with that I became totally undone and collapsed on the couch. Before I could even catch my breath he stuck his dick in me and began pumping in and out so slowly I was losing my fucking mind.

"Damn ma this shit is wet and tight as hell, I'm not sure how long I'm going to be able to hold out." "Tell me that this pussy is mine Kam."

"Mhmmm its yours."

"What's my name Kam? Say my name baby."

"J, Jamil this pussy is yours baby, I'm gonna cum." "Shit girl me too," and after a couple more pumps we both came at the same time.

Now we're supposed to be talking about what's going to happen with us but a bitch needed a nap first after that bomb ass sex we just had so we both ended up falling asleep. About two hours later I woke up to relieve my bladder and to freshen up, afterwards I woke Jamil up so we can finally have a much needed talk.

"So J, I've been doing some thinking and I've decided that I want to continue this relationship that we have, but I'm nervous J, like really nervous."

"Baby I understand that and trust me a nigga ain't trying to purposely hurt you but I'm glad you sticking with a nigga. I'm not going to lie to you Kam but things may get rough for us but please don't turn your back on me, I've had too many people turn their backs on me in my life."

"As long as you got me then I got you J, I love you."

. . .

"I love you too and I promise you got me Kam and we going to be good."

For the rest of the night we just laid around watching tv and talking about all types of stuff including our relationship. I really hope I don't regret this.

NINETEEN

MORE THAN LIKELY you guys are judging me because I decided to still mess with him knowing he's married and after that shit Tatiana pulled on me I shouldn't be doing the same thing to another woman. Granted your all right but at the same time I didnt even know he was married at first and I don't owe any loyalty to his wife. It's fucked up honestly but it's the truth. Tatiana's hoe ass knew what it was but still chose to do it. This is definitely something I would never do again but unfortunately I can't take it back now.

Things with me and J have been going pretty good. It's basically the same way it was before I found out about the wife. We still have our monthly dates sometimes twice a month, we've still been taking little weekend trips. He's still always there when I need him to be well for the most part. I still don't think us still messing around is a good thing but the heart wants what it wants right. It's even gotten to the point to where he even sleeps in a different room when he's home. I do think the wife is trying hard to make it work with them because she's been calling him a lot more and she tries to keep him home more, trying to say the kids need something all time. It makes me worry that her efforts may work and he may end completely leaving me alone and I'll end up heart broken again.

As I'm sitting here watching a movie with my baby girl I hear the doorbell ring, since Quran was coming by to pick up Summer, I didn't even bothering looking out of the peephole but I wish I would have because when I did I had an unexpected visitor.

"Bitch didn't I tell ya fat ass to stay away from my husband!" I don't understand why these bitches have to keep coming for my weight when obviously I'm still getting they dudes no matter what.

"Well obviously your husband likes my fat ass since he can't seem to leave me alone. Now when I said that this bitch decides she wants to hit me, so of course I had to hit her ass back. Now we outside on my porch going at it, my nose is leaking her eye is swollen and we managed to roll off the porch onto the damn grass.

As I was banging her head into the grass I was suddenly snatched away from her. "Kam what the hell is going on?" Quran shouted at me. Nice of him to show up at this exact moment.

"Well baby daddy if you must know this is my boyfriend's wife and she's mad because her husband still wants to fuck with me even after he got caught." He just stood there shaking his head at me. "You know your better than this baby momma." He was absolutely right but at the same time ain't no way a bitch was going to swing on me and wasn't going to shoot the fair one. Ain't no bitch in my blood. "Qu you know ain't no way I'm just gonna let a bitch hit on me and I not do anything back."

"I hear you Kam but can you go in the house now so I can get the baby and get out of here, your nose is bleeding and shit." When we walked in the house Quran went and got something for me to clean up my nose. I just stood there and started crying because this is not what I signed up for. I love Jamil but I'm not fit to be fighting anybody, At the end of the day we can fight a thousand times but if he still wants to be with both of us he still will until one of us stops it. Quran walked backed into the room and handed me the washcloth and noticed me crying, so he reached out to hug me. "Aww babygirl I know I fucked up what we had but you don't deserve this. Your a beautiful woman and you shouldn't play second to anyone. Don't let this nigga or no other nigga including me make you come down off your throne. Your a queen baby and don't let nobody tell you otherwise."

Later on that night as I sat there reflecting on everything that has transpired I thought it maybe a good idea to leave Jamil alone for good. To have his wife show up at my door on some rah rah shit isn't something I'm used to. The outcome of that whole situation could have been totally different. One of us could have been seriously hurt and over what a dude. Nah I'm not trying to go out like that.

I was so deep in my thoughts that I didn't hear the doorbell ring or the door actually being opened with a key until I saw Jamil entering my living room out the corner of my eye.

"What's good baby? I rang the doorbell first but since you didn't answer so I used my key."

"What's good you ask me? Should I tell you what's not good, how about the fact that your wife came to my damn house, where my child is at and wanted to fight me."

"I'm sorry about that, I had no idea she was going to do that, and I didn't find out until a few minutes ago before I came over here."

"My question is how the fuck does she know where I even live at?" At this point I'm standing directly in his face pointing my finger at his chest.

"Ma I swear I don't know how she knows that, maybe she followed me or something but I know I never told her bae, you have to believe me."

"That's besides the point now J, what if something far worse than a little black eye or a busted nose would have happened. Technically I could have killed her and got away with it since she was on my property."

"I know and I said that to her. I can promise you I have everything under control and it won't happen again" he said while pulling me into his arms.

Needless to say I was dumb enough to believe him and the minute he began kissing on my neck and rubbing all over my body, the thoughts of leaving him when straight out the window. Let's just say for the rest of the night he made love to me and made me forget the craziness of earlier.

The next morning I woke up and J wasn't there. I figured he went home sometime while I was sleep but then I smelled bacon cooking. Let me find out he was making me breakfast. I got up to handle my hygiene and when I came out the room it was a tray on the bed with flowers and breakfast. "Aww babe is this for me."

"Yeah I just wanted to show you I was sorry for what went on yesterday and I will do anything in my power for nothing like that to happen again.

"Thanks bae, I definitely do appreciate it," I said to him while dancing in my seat. Food always makes me happy. Shit I'm fat, don't judge me.

TWENTY

AFTER THAT INCIDENT with the wife, things with J and I were pretty good for the most part. Our relationship continued on for a couple more years after that but it wasn't easy. There was another time the wife showed up but this time I didn't even bother opening my door. I was not about to keep fighting over a man, especially because he was going to continue doing what he wanted to do. Since she couldn't get to me she flattened my tires on my truck. I just called the police on her ass and pressed charges, bitch I'm too old and too fat to keep tussling with a bitch in the streets. One day when Gabi and I were out having lunch when we saw them together in a restaurant with their children and she actually walked up to my table and was like "are you still fucking my husband?" My response, "ask ya husband." Again I'm not about to doing this shit especially in a restaurant while I'm trying to eat. I guess my answer was good enough or maybe it wasn't but who the fuck cares but she just walked away after that.

I do feel like things are slowly coming to an end with us because he's changed a little. He doesn't come over as much, we haven't went on a trip in a while and even though we still have went on a few dates it just isn't the same. To be honest it's probably a good thing that it is coming to an end since it wasn't supposed to happen in the first place and definitely not last this long. I could have potentially missed out on my future husband because anybody that tried to talk to me I turned them down. I mean I was getting treated good even if it was with someone else's husband. Hopefully one day this karma doesn't come back on me because I really didn't set out to mess with some-one's husband. The shit just happened, well sort of considering he didn't tell me. Today he and I are supposed to meet up for lunch so let me go get myself ready.

A few hours later I ended up at some local pizzeria and Jamil was already there. I was totally not prepared for the conversation that transpired.

"Hey Kam" he said to me while hugging me.

"Hi Jamil, how are you?" "I'm good, I asked you to come here because I wanted to talk to you about something." I just sat there and gave him a look like okay I'm listening. "You know I love you right?" Oh boy I thought to myself, it's about to be some bullshit. Anytime a nigga start a sentence off like that it means ain't nothing but bad news to follow. "Yes Jamil I know you do but why would you ask me that?"

. . .

"Listen Kam there is no way other to put this but we have to end this ma. You mean the world to me and you have helped me become a better man but I have to try and work out my marriage at least for my kids sake. They see us arguing all the time and it's beginning to take a toll on them. Hell all of this is taking a toll on me. I hope ya understand that." Now I'm sitting here just looking at him like he's lost his damn mind. Granted deep down I understand what he's saying but do I like it? Hell no! I knew sooner or later I would get my feelings hurt but I just didn't expect it like this. I mean shit wasn't he the one trying his best to get me stay, wasn't he the one saying don't turn my back on him what does he do turn his back on me. What type of shit is that!? "Kam, Kam, you not going to say anything?" he asked me bringing me out of my thoughts. At this point the tears are falling and I couldn't stop them if I wanted to. I want him to see how he's hurt me, the same one who claimed he was different from my daughter's father. The hurt I feel now is way worse than the hurt that I felt with Quran. Finally I decided to respond to him. "Jamil how can you sit here and tell me this shit after you told me don't turn my back on you but clearly you are turning your back on me." I have put up with your damn wife trying to fight me, vandalizing my shit and everything but I still stayed and now all of a sudden you want to up and leave me well FUCK YOU! I screamed and threw my cup of water on him. Everything was getting blurry from me crying so much and I just had to get the hell out of there. When your marriage still doesn't work out don't you dare hit my line because I can't be there for you anymore. Have a nice life and with my head held high I left that pizza place. The sad part is I was so hurt I never got to eat my damn food.

After what seemed like forever I finally made it home. It took me a little longer because I had to pull over a couple of times and get myself together. Thank goodness the baby was with Quran because lord knows I can't deal with no children right now. I think I'm gonna take a nice hot bath and drink some tea since both of those things usually calm me down. Putting on some music, I got in the tub and let the music say how I was feeling. When "I Care" by Beyoncé came on I swear this song was speaking to my soul. I sat in that tub crying my eyes out and singing the song like I was Beyonce.

I told you how you hurt me, baby
But you don't care
Now I'm crying and deserted, baby
But you don't care

Do I think that J doesn't care? As a matter of fact right now I damn sure don't think he cares. Only someone who doesn't care can hurt you the way he's hurt me. I never thought being heartbroken can cause physical pain. It literally feels like there is a hole in my heart right now. There is legit pain in my chest and I hope I never feel this pain ever again in life and I hope I never cause anyone this type of pain. I don't know how long I've been sitting in this tub and listening to the same song over and over again but I told myself I'm only allowing myself two days tops to wallow in my sorrows. Even though this hurts more than when Quran hurt me, I refuse to allow someone to have so much power over my emotions. I have a child to take care of and school to finish and they both are much more important than some broken heart. Shit it's not the first one and who knows it may not be the last time.

TWENTY-ONE

FOR THE LAST year I've just been focusing on myself and my daughter. I'm close to finally graduating with my PHD in psychology and my baby girl is getting so big. Even though Quran ain't shit he has been a damn good father to her. He's even been there for me even when I don't want him to be. For instance the one time he came over and I was just having a bad day and crying and before you know it him comforting me turned into him fucking me right on my kitchen counter. Do I regret it? Hell no. Shit I had him first and I was horny so why not get it from someone you knew, no need to add more to my body count, even though it was only two but you never know when you may have a whorish moment. Back to my point, he knew wasn't nothing going to come out of it. Hell he's still with Tati and she's pregnant again. I think this is baby number two or three, shit I can't keep up. Better her than me.

I did manage to go on a couple of dates but it wasn't nobody special enough to mention. There was this one guy that I wasn't even sure if he was a guy or not. As we were sitting there eating this nigga starts choking so I had to do the Heimlich maneuver on him and let's just say that was the end of the date. Then there was the guy in the grocery store that would be working in the cereal aisle and would just stare at me every time I went in there. Well he finally built up the courage to ask me on a date and at first I was going to say yeah but I noticed his butt was a little too big so I had to kindly decline. We both can't be out here with fat asses. Let's just say I got tired of the dating world pretty quick.

Today I was going to meet up with my girls for dinner and drinks and catch up with what's been going on with them. Tonight's pick was this restaurant/hookah bar called Taurus lounge. It was a nice little chill spot. They had some bomb ass food and you can smoke hookah. It was the best of both worlds. Anyway I was feeling myself tonight. I was rocking a flower print romper and some wedged heels. My heels always have to have a wedged heel. Shit I need something to hold my weight. Walking in I noticed Gabi and Keysha was already sitting at a table. Damn I'm always late, I'll probably be the one late to my wedding or hell maybe my own funeral.

"What's up bitches!"

"Hey late ass" Gabi said laughing at me.

"For real Kam why are you always late?" Keysha questioned.

"Um because I'm single and I had to make sure my shit was on point since you never know who your going to run into. You never know I can meet my future husband tonight."

"Bitch you were late even when you were in a relationship so don't try it."

"Gab you tried it but anyway what's been up with y'all?"

Before either one of them answered I noticed two figures out of the corner of my eye and guess who the hell it was. Jamil and his damn wife. Now I'm going to pretend I don't see either one of them and let's hope they do the same and we all can enjoy our night. Of course just like any other time that thought was short lived because sure as shit her ass had to come walking her way to my damn table.

"Hey fat bitch how does it feel knowing you didn't last long. I guess you weren't woman enough for him since he stayed with me."

A part of me thought about ignoring her ass but I felt like being a little petty tonight since I got over him, well sort of but her or him will never know that.

"Obviously Ya Husband thought my fat ass was woman enough if he stayed with me as long as he did. Maybe you should be asking yourself if you were woman enough since he cheated on you with my Fat Ass! The only reason why he tried to work it out with ya dumb ass is because of the kids. So instead of trying to bash me every chance you get maybe you should be trying to figure out why he cheated in the first place. Now if you would be so kind and get the fuck away from my table, oh and tell J I said hi. She just stood there for a minute looking dumb then turned and walked away. I just don't understand why females always have to approach the female in those situations. Now if I knew her or even knew about her then the situation would be different but that's not the case. Maybe she should try to find out why her husband isn't or wasn't wearing his ring or why he failed to mention he had a wife in the first place. Trying to fight me every time she sees me is not going to change anything. Whatever problems they have are still going to be there. Let me get back to my girls.

"So like I asked before I was rudely interrupted, what's going on with y'all?"

"Well Kam my dude has a homeboy that works with him and he saw a picture of you and wants to meet you."

"Keysha have you seen him before or are you just going off what ya dude said."

"Nah I seen him, he's cute and he even has a beard like you like. Shit maybe you should stay away from beards since the last two with beards turned out to be shit."

"You might be right Keysha but what's his name?" Thinking to myself I may not be ready to be in a whole relationship but what's wrong with having a little friend. Shit the weather is getting nice and I wouldn't mind going on some dates. She went on to tell me his name is Tyson and since he's a bouncer he has a little money coming in. I threw caution to the wind and told her to give him my number. For the rest of the night we just enjoyed ourselves with some hookah and drinks flowing. I was living my best life. Every once in a while I would notice Jamil looking at me and apparently his wife noticed too because she got mad and they started arguing and eventually left. Oh well sucks for them.

A couple of days later while I was lounging around the house my cell phone rings. "Hello" I answered. "Yeah is this Kamaya?" "This is she, may I ask who's calling?" "This is Tyson, ya home girl Keysha gave me your number a couple of days ago and I finally had a chance to call you." Now for a hot second I forgot even agreeing to give him my number but his voice sounded so low and deep. Like tell me a bedtime story and I'll fall asleep deep so I was definitely intrigued.

"Hey how are you?" I asked him. "I'm good but I was wondering if you wanted to go to Chipotle with me for a light dinner tonight, I know it's last minute but I'm free and I was hoping maybe you were too." How do I tell him I don't even like Chipotle without possibly hurting his feelings, you know dudes is sensitive these days. Y'all probably are thinking since I'm chunky that I eat any and everything, well guess what y'all wrong because I'm picky as hell. "Sure, most likely I'll be available later, I'll give you a call in a few hours." Okay cool he said, I'm looking forward to officially meeting you. Needless to say I fell asleep on the couch and I didn't wake up until the next morning so I never went anywhere, hell I didn't even call the dude back. I doubt he was too worried about me anyway.

Getting up to get my day started I heard my house phone ring, yeah people still have those. The only people that call me on it are Keysha and Gabi and occasionally Quran. My cell phone must have died since I slept on the couch and never charged it. I guess that's why someone was calling the house. I went in the kitchen to answer it. "Jones residence," I had to sound all proper just in case it was of importance. "Girl! How come you never called Tyson back?" Keysha asked me. "He was all upset like ya girl stood me up, blah, blah, blah, I think you hurt that man feelings." Laughing I told her I had fell asleep that's why I didn't call him and maybe I'll try to call him later. Please do she said, because I don't want to hear his whining. He don't even know you and acting like that already. "Chile I'll call him," I said to her and hung up. To some that may have been a red flag but we all know sometimes we tend to ignore those flags and that's exactly what I did and I will live to regret it.

TWENTY-TWO

SO YOU KNOW those situations where ya new dude or chick ex tell you some not so great things about them but you don't always listen because in your mind your like your the ex of course your going to say some bad stuff. Well let me tell ya that that's not always the case. So apparently Tyson's ex works with Gabrielle and she told her some not so good things about him. He's apparently a manipulator, a liar and a thief. Now of course I didn't want to believe her since she could be the bitter ex or maybe he was but people change so maybe he wouldn't be like that with me but boy was I wrong. Let me rewind some and tell y'all how I found all this out.

Since I kind of stood Tyson up and I was bored I decided to give him a call and see if maybe we can try again. Picking up my cell phone I dialed his number.

"Hello is this Tyson?" "Yeah what's good who is this?" Now I don't know if he didn't store my number or he was still salty because more than likely he knew who it was but I decided to play along. "Hi Tyson this is Kamaya and I wanted to first apologize about the other night and I wanted to see if we can try again."

"Sure that's cool, did you have anything in mind, we can still hit up Chipotle if you want."

"Actually I don't eat Mexican food but maybe we can go get some ice cream and maybe go to this little area I know on the other side of town. They have nice scenery and a couple of different stores and stuff and maybe we can just walk around a little."

"I'm with it shorty but I'm at my people's crib right now so do you think you can pick me up?" "Sure no problem, shoot me the address" I told him. For some people this needing a ride may be another red flag. It's like does he even have a car or not. My thought is since he's out with his people's maybe one of them picked him up. Who knows but I will definitely inquire about that. A little while later I decided to go pick him up. Since it was nice and I wanted to walk a little I put on some jean capris, a blue shirt and some blue huaraches. Gotta be cute and comfortable. While I was driving to the address he sent my phone rang through my car speakers. Looking at the caller ID I noticed it was Jamil calling me, I'm thinking to myself what the hell does he want? Should I answer or not? After the 4th ring my curiosity got the best of me and I decided to answer. "Hello Jamil how can I help you?"

"Damn Kamaya why do you have to be so formal?, a nigga was just calling to check up on you and to hear your voice." "We were friends as well so it's nothing wrong with me checking up on a friend right?"

"Yes J we were friends but I don't think your wife would like you calling me so I'm good, thanks for checking on me and you take care," and with that I hung up on his ass. I was not going to allow him the opportunity to talk me out of my draws if that's what he thought he was going to do. Plus I had arrived at my destination. It was a lot of cars out here so I had trouble finding somewhere to park so I drove up the street a little and called him. I wasn't sure what to expect since this was my first time actually meeting him and when I saw him coming up the street my ass almost pulled off. This fool had on these white and blue stripe pants like he played baseball and a white and blue shirt that had stars on it, oh and I forgot the weird looking sneakers he had on that just didn't go with the outfit at all. Just throw the whole damn outfit away. They say don't judge a book by its cover but it's hard not to with someone dressed the way he was. I decided though to officially meet him and see what happens. Now if we end up in a relationship I will definitely be helping him upgrade his wardrobe.

He finally made it to the car and I must say he was handsome and he had a nice beard. We all know I'm a sucka for a nice beard. Anyway once I drove off we officially introduced ourselves and made idle chatter. He informed me that he did have a car but he rode with one of his boys to the place he was at. He's been working in security for a little while and he owns his own home. He seemed to have something going for himself but the words of his ex kind of danced around in my head. For all I know this fool could be lying. Only time will tell. I went on to tell him a little bit about myself as well.

Arriving at our destination he got out and opened my door for me. Hmm a gentleman, maybe chivalry isn't dead or his could just be trying to get some brownie points. He even grabbed my hand as we started walking.

"So sweetheart is there anywhere in particular you want to go while we are out here?" "Sure is," I told him, I wanted to get some ice cream. We proceeded to the ice cream place and when it was time to pay he offered to pay and of course I wasn't going to refuse. We decided on just walking around the area and at one point he even wiped a little ice cream off my face. I thought it was cute. I noticed a group of girls walking our way and he was staring a little too hard. Now ain't nothing wrong with looking but when your with someone whether it's a girlfriend or just a date you should show some respect and his ass damn near broke his neck looking at them. So another possible red flag.

I decided to let that little situation slide and enjoyed the rest of the date. We just continued to walk and get to know each other. I found out he didn't live too far from me, and he has two sons and that he's very active in their lives. Supposedly him and their mother get along well so we shouldn't have any baby momma drama. He also informed me that he wanted to start his own security firm, which I think would be a good idea. I told him that I wanted to open my own practice so I hope he's not saying stuff because he thinks that's what I want to hear. I can't stand when people, especially dudes, tell you stuff that they think you want to hear instead of just being honest about things. I've had enough liars in my life, I really can't deal with anymore. I may mess around kill the next person to lie to me. Why is it so hard for people to be honest and just say how they feel about things? Maybe I expect too much from people since I'm always open and honest with them.

We ended up enjoying each other's company so much that neither one of us wanted the date to end so soon so we decided to go see what Fallon and her dude were up to. For hours we all just laughed and joked and played different games. We even discussed going on a double date in the near future.

TWENTY-THREE

SO A FEW WEEKS have gone by and Tyson and I have went on a few dates and I'm really enjoying his carefree lifestyle. He does a lot of things without thinking of the consequences but so far it's nothing crazy so it hasn't bothered me. I'm learning to live a little day by day instead of trying to plan everything out. He does always have these grandiose ideas and sometimes I think he says certain things because he thinks I want to hear it. For instance one day we were having a conversation about things we want in our futures and I mentioned about possibly moving to another state and getting married one day. Coincidentally he said he wanted the same thing but I'm not completely convinced. Sometimes you can just tell when someone isn't being completely genuine. Who knows though, I guess I'll just wait and see what happens.

Tonight we were going out to dinner and a movie. As soon as I finished getting dressed I heard a horn beep. Now I'm thinking to myself I know this nigga has more manners than that. You don't beep no horn for a real woman, your supposed to be a gentleman and come and ring the doorbell. I damn sure was going to say something about that as soon as I got to the car. Locking up my house and walking to the car, this fool didn't even get out to open my door or nothing. To me that was rude or maybe because I was so used to Jamil always opening doors for me. Oh well let me go and hopefully enjoy this date.

"Hello Tyson, how are you?" I asked him while putting on my seatbelt. He was looking all good and shit so I wasn't going to stress over the door situation. He had on this blue polo with some dark denim jeans and some Flight Club Jordan's.

"I'm good sweetheart, how is life treating you?"

"I'm doing pretty good, I told him. But listen you do know that you are supposed to get out and ring the doorbell when you pick a woman up from her house, as well as opening the car door for her. I mean that is the gentleman thing to do."

"You know what shorty you right and that's my bad, that won't happen again," he told me while licking his juicy ass lips.

"I'll forgive you this time," I chuckled. There was no need to be too hard on him but you have to let these dudes know what you want and expect in the beginning. A man is only going to treat you the way you allow him. Some of these chicks don't know what to do with a gentleman so theses guys don't be acting like one.

"Cool little lady, now let's go and enjoy the rest of our date."

We decided on having dinner at Applebee's. After eating and

having a few drinks I got a little tipsy and considered skipping the movie because more than likely I would fall asleep watching it. As if he was reading my mind Tyson suggested we go get a room somewhere to chill. He claimed we were kinda far from his house and since he was drinking too he didn't want to drive to my house either. Apparently there was a motel nearby so that's where we ended up at. Now here's where the first real problem occurred. He never went to the front desk to pay or get keys to a room, he just started turning knobs to see which one opened. In my mind I'm thinking this is a bad idea but I'm not saying anything.

After he tried a few doors one finally opened. "Come on girl this one opened," he whispered to me. I looked at this fool like he was crazy but I decided to throw caution to the wind, plus I was a little tipsy so I said fuck it and went in. The room looked clean so I'm guessing it was cleaned for the next paying guest. We in the room just chillin, of course I'm nervous as hell hoping the cops don't come or something and this fool is acting like he paid for the shit. He done took his shirt and shoes off, you know real comfortable like. Anyway he starts trying to kiss me and I figured why not loosen up a little so I kiss him back. He starts rubbing on my breast and I'm thinking that tonight might just be the night I give him some, well as soon as he gets my pants down there is this sudden noise at the door. At this point I'm freaking out, I'm out here ass out in an unpaid room and now the cops are coming to lock my ass up. After my mini freak out I rushed into the bathroom to put my clothes back on and this joker is laughing. Once we get outside there is this Mexican couple looking a little upset that they couldn't get into the room they paid for. When we made it to the car and I realized the cops wasn't coming I finally let out the breath I was holding and I started cracking up.

Since that was a dud we ended up just going back to my place, which we should have done from the beginning. "How about we finish what we started back at the room" Tyson said to me while trying to take my top off. I'm not even going to get into all that happened because let's just say even though he had a lot to work with but there was no intimacy whatsoever. He barely even wanted to do foreplay. Now everyone knows you have to warm a female up before sex.

After the mediocre sex we just laid there talking about different things we wanted out of life. Now you may be asking why did I let him stay after the lackluster sex but it was because we had a good vibe and two his dick was big, like 9 inches big so I may just have to teach him a few things. Sometimes you have to throw your teacher's hat on and show them what you need and want. This was the first of many nights he stayed over. Now that I think about it I don't think his ass ever left after that night. So since he never really left I started to think that maybe he didn't have his own place, because if he did why would he want to be at my house so much.

A couple of days later while we were out he says to me "Kam let's stop by my house real quick" "Sure no problem," I told him. About twenty minutes later we ended up at his house and he offered me inside. I noticed that we were going to the side of the house instead of the front door but I didn't think too much about it. Anyway we go inside and he takes me to the basement. An unfinished basement at that, so I'm standing in the middle of the room and it's surrounded by all types of stuff. So I'm wondering why we are down here when my thoughts are interrupted by him kissing me and he starts rubbing on my ass. In my mind I'm like I know he isn't about to try and fuck me in this basement but I like spontaneity so I said fuck it and went along with it. So after we got our clothes off and got into it, I hear a woman calling his name. In my mind I'm hoping I hope this nigga don't have a wife or girl he didn't tell me about. "Nigga I know you didn't bring me to no house you share with a bitch!" Before he could respond, I hear the woman yell out "Tyson I know you don't have some bitch in my house!" "See what's not about to happen is some bitch I have no clue about calling me out of my name," I said to him. "Nah baby it's not like that, this is my mother's house and I just happen to live here." "Tyson why didn't you say that shit in the beginning?" "Because Kam I know if I would have said I live with my mom more than likely you would have cut that date short." He did have a point but I wasn't going to tell him that though. Now I like him so I'm not going to hold it against him. "That may very well be true but you wouldn't know because you didn't say anything. I'm not tripping though, but just be honest about things with me." He went to go talk to his mother and I got dressed and snuck my ass back out the way I came in. I wasn't trying to meet his mom under those circumstances.

TWENTY-FOUR

NEEDLESS TO SAY Tyson kind of just moved himself into my house. I didn't trip off it because I actually liked having him there. He was very clean and he would cook me dinner almost everyday. So there was that benefit. The only problem is Summer Reign wasn't too thrilled with him being there. She usually likes everyone but it was something about him that she didn't like. She was only 5 years old so I thought maybe she just needed some time to get used to him. Today when I came home from work there was a cute little shihtzu puppy waiting for me at the door. "Hey little guy," I said to the puppy picking him up and he just started licking my face. Aww your so cute, I'm going to call you Gucci. Going into the kitchen Tyson was at the stove cooking dinner, and I just stood there appreciating the fact that he was doing that for me. It's hard these days for a dude to cook and clean for you. I guess after a few minutes he felt my presence because he turned around and smiled at me. "Hey baby" he said walking towards me. "Hi Tyson, I see you in here whipping it up." "Yeah you know how I do but how was your day?" He even had one of my aprons on. "My day was long and stressful but I'm glad it's over." "Well don't worry your pretty little head, I ran you some bath water and by the time you get done the dinner will be ready, and I'll even rub your feet for you." "Aww thank you baby," I said to him and kissed him on his lips. When I turned to leave the kitchen he smacked me on my ass and said "no problem ma."

That bath was everything, I stayed in there for about 30 minutes until Tyson came told me that the dinner was ready. We haven't had sex in a while because sometimes he be acting like he don't want to do it. Not sure what that's about but tonight I'm going to try. The last time I tried he straight up turned me down, like damn who's the chick in the relationship. Any other person I've been with I didn't even have to ask for it because they were always over me. Anyway a bitch got needs so I'm shooting my shot after dinner. This is one of the things that bother me about him though. Like either you on some other shit or your fucking another bitch and if he's doing that he can get his ass up out here. I figured I'll give him something to look at while we eat so I put on some lingerie and some heels. I came out the room to candles lit everywhere and in the kitchen it was a candlelight dinner for two.

. . .

"Wow babe all this for me?" I asked Tyson. "Yes it's all for you. I see how you've been busy trying to get your practice together and everything else and I just wanted to do something special for you. So tonight is all about you. Sit down relax and I'll get your plate." "Thank you and I appreciate you," I told him. For dinner we had my favorite, BBQ chicken, baked macaroni and cheese, and cornbread. He even made some red kool aid and baked a cake. I wonder if he's up to something. After we ate dinner we went into the living room to watch a movie and relax. The whole time the movie was on he massaged my feet and I felt so relaxed I started dozing off. Eventually I woke up to him kissing on my neck.

Once I fully woke up he began kissing me and I can taste the mint he must have just ate. He started rubbing his hands over my breast. "Kamaya you are so fucking sexy, can I make love to you tonight?" Well damn we went from barely doing it to him talking about making love. Hell yeah I was with it. "Yes you can make love to me," I breathed out. He took one of my breast out of the top of my lingerie and began sucking on it. He suddenly stopped, "what you stop for?" "I was just going to turn the lights off," he said. "No leave the lights on, let's try something new tonight." "Well shit girl show me what you trying to do." We began kissing again and I started to take his pants off for him. I had some caramel sauce so I poured some of that on his dick. I began slowly licking it off of him. "Damn ma," was all he said. Once I licked it up I put his whole dick in my mouth until it hit the back of my throat. He began pulling my hair and I gagged on his dick a couple of times making my mouth water. "Sss, damn this shit feels good," he said still pulling my hair. After a few more minutes I got up and sat on his dick, there was no way he was going to get that nut and I wasn't. I had to ease down on it because he's kinda big and since we don't do it that much it's probably going to hurt. Once I got it all the way in, I began riding it nice and slow.

. . .

After I started speeding up he grabbed me by wrist and began slapping me on my ass. "Yeah girl come all over this dick," and after a few more pumps I did just that. He then flipped me over and began hitting it from the back and pulling my hair. He was going so deep I couldn't help but to holler out. Luckily the baby wasn't here so I don't have to worry about making too much noise and waking her up. I got to do all the hollering I wanted and I damn sure did. About 10 pumps later I felt his dick get harder and he started speeding up so I knew he was about to cum so I made sure I came right with him. "Whew, damn girl that was everything," he said kissing me on the back of my neck. "Come on let's go to bed," he said helping me up off the couch.

The next day I got up before he did so I went to clean up everything and make breakfast. The smell of bacon must have woke Tyson up because once I started making it he came into the kitchen. "Good morning," he said coming in with just some basketball shorts on and no shirt. "Good morning, breakfast is almost done," I told him. "Cool, cool, there's something I want to talk to you about once we sit down and eat." Yeah that's fine, I told him and continued to make breakfast. I only made some cheese eggs, bacon and toast. I really wasn't that hungry so I didn't want to make a lot of food and it go to waste.

I sat down across from Tyson at the table once I made both of our plates and poured us some apple juice. "So Kam I was thinking that maybe we should open a joint bank account so we can have money for the bills and things around the house. We both put a little in every time we get paid and every month we'll pay some bills with it or maybe take a trip or something." Now I had to think about this for a second because I'm not sure if we were ready for a joint account. Well I knew I was capable of it but I wasn't sure if he was but I gave it a shot. "Yeah I think we can do that."

. . .

A couple of weeks later I noticed that I didn't get this check that I've been waiting for so I decided to call them and see what was going on with it. I couldn't believe it when she told me it was cashed already. Now I know I'm not tripping because I never seen the check. After she told me multiple times that it was cashed, I finally hung up the phone. My next step was to check the new account we just and sure as shit the thing was closed already but I was able to see that this bastard stole my check and deposited it and never bothered to tell me. So I'm sitting here in disbelief that he actually stole from me. Let me call his ass right now and see what kind of bullshit he says. "Mutha-fucka you stole from me!" I screamed as soon as he answered the phone.

TWENTY-FIVE

"WOAH, woah, Kam what are you talking about? Who stole what?" So I guess he gonna sit here and play stupid like I don't know he stole my shit. There hasn't been anybody else in here so I know for a fact it was him. "You nigga, that's who! You stole the fucking check I've been waiting for. Why you would do something like that to me of all people?" My voice was starting to become shaky because I was so angry I was on the verge of tears. One thing I don't like is someone stealing from me. He knows damn well if he needed something I would have given it to him. Maybe Summer not liking him was a sign I should have paid attention to.

"Ma it wasn't even like that. I went to put it in the bank for you but then I had this opportunity to flip it so I did it. The plan was to make double the money back and put it in the bank before you even got a chance to notice it missing. I wouldn't just steal from you like that baby. I was trying to make some money for both of us." He said all this shit like it's supposed to make up for the fact of him stealing. "I don't give a fuck what you were trying to do Tyson you still don't steal from ya girl!" "But Kam don't think of like that, it was an investment for our future." I had to pull the phone away from my ear and just look at it because he really was talking crazy.

"Listen Tyson I get what your saying and I understand what you were trying to do but you just don't take someone's money regardless of what it was for. You should have just come to me and told me what you wanted to do instead of stealing from me. Not only did you steal from me but technically you stole from my daughter as well." I can't believe he is really acting like he didn't do anything wrong. How can I trust him in my house if he can steal from me like that. Who knows what else he'll do. "Kamaya I'm sorry I did that but I would never intentionally do anything to hurt. That was a bad judgment call on my part and I truly apologize. I promise you nothing like that will ever happen again. I will also give you every last dime back. Do you forgive me?" I'm not even sure if I should forgive him and is he really going to give me the money back, who knows. "As of right now I can't say that I forgive you but I definitely will need my money back and nothing like this can ever happen again." "I got you Kam and again I apologize," he said to be sounding remorseful but I'm not convinced that he is. "I'll just talk to you later Tyson." "Okay baby I love you," he said but I just hung up on him. I couldn't even tell him I loved him back because I was still so pissed off.

. . .

I needed someone to talk to so I decided to give Gabi a call. I know she'll talk some sense into me about this situation. "Bitch let me tell," I said to her as soon as she answered the phone. You know a bitch got some tea to spill when she starts a sentence off like that. "Damn hello to you to Kam," she said. "My bad, hi Gabi but let me tell you what happened. So you know that check I've been waiting for?" Before she even had a chance to respond I started telling her how Tyson stole it and the bullshit excuse as to why he did it. "Bitch I know you lying!" She screamed into the phone. "Where is his bitch ass at, I'm going to fuck him up!" See that's the thing about Gabi she always be ready to fight somebody, Keysha on the other hand is always the voice of reason so depending on what kind of advice I want and need determines which one I call first. Either way they both find out everything but it's usually one before the other. "I hope his ass is somewhere trying to get my damn money back." I continued to talk to Gabi a little longer and we decided to meet up soon. It seems like its been a while since we had a girls night out and I definitely can use one.

Tonight was girls night. We were going to pregame at my house so I made a little quick dinner and I got us some drinks. I made us some strawberry daiquiris and we had chicken and broccoli alfredo with garlic bread. Tyson and I had kind of gotten over the whole check fiasco and things were going okay. He still hasn't giving me a dime of the money back and I'm starting to think he probably won't. For now though I'm going to push all the negative thoughts to the side and focus on having fun with my girls.

We decided on going to our usual spot Club Fetish, and unfortunately Tyson was working there tonight as well as Keysha's boyfriend. I hope Tyson don't be on his bullshit and be worrying about what I got going on. Walking into the club I noticed Jamil's wife there and she noticed me too because she was eyeballing the shit out of me. From what I've been hearing things with them haven't been going to well and she blames me for it even though its been years since I dealt with him. Hopefully she goes on about her business so I can go about mine. She walked past and bumped into me but I decided to just let go. It wasn't until she came back again and decided she wanted to say something to me. "Hey fat ass." It's like no matter what this bitch always have to say something. You would think after all this time she would be over the shit but apparently not. "Fuck you ugly bitch," I said back then turned to walk away.

For the rest of the night my girls and I tore that club up. Even Tyson came over to dance with me when he had a little break. He also got mad though when he seen a couple of guys trying to talk to me and buy me drinks. I entertained them for a little bit but not for too long. Didn't want to cause any unnecessary drama. Even though Tyson be on his bullshit sometimes I'm still in a relationship so I chatted for a little bit and kept it pushing.

I was feeling the music and dancing my little heart out when I felt someone wrap their arms around my waist. "Hey beautiful in about five minutes me in the bathroom upstairs." I was surprised he said that and since I was tipsy and our sex life is usually kind of vanilla, I got excited by his wanting to be spontaneous for a change. I waited the five minutes and let Gabi and Keysha know where I was going. When I got in the bathroom Tyson was already in there. As soon as I closed and locked the door he was all over me. "Damn baby you looking good tonight and I couldn't wait until later when we got home, I had to have you now. I don't have that much time so we have to make this quick." He didn't have to tell me twice plus I didn't want to be in here too long anyway and have the girls come looking for me. Before I can have seconds thoughts about this he turned me around and pushed me against the sink, lifted my dress and slammed his dick in me. "Fuck ma, you was ready for a nigga huh" he whispered in my ear. After he went a few more strokes we were done and he kissed me on the cheek and left. He had to get back to work. I cleaned myself up and left the bathroom to go find the girls.

"Damn Kam did you fall in?" Gabi asked me. "No I didn't fall in, Tyson and I had a little quickie in the bathroom." I told them sticking out my tongue. Okay bihh! they both said at the same time. "Yeah it was spontaneous so it caught me off guard. Our sex is usually kind of boring so it was fun doing something different." "Hey if you like it we love it," Keysha said. We ended up staying until the club closed. Tonight was definitely a good night and hopefully when Tyson comes home we can go for round two.

TWENTY-SIX

LET'S just say the stolen check wasn't the only issue with Tyson. A couple of weeks later he told me we were going to a friends party. So of course I had to be fly. I decided to go buy a new outfit. This would be the first time we would be around his friends so I wanted to make sure my shit was on point. I ended up going by myself instead of calling the girls. Both of them were at work plus I can use some alone time.

It seems like whenever I'm just trying to have a relaxing day someone is always around to disrupt my peace. Heading to the food court I saw two people I really didn't want to see but there they were sitting there like a happy couple. "Well if it isn't my baby daddy and my former best friend, it's good to see you guys are still together. "Hey Tati your looking fat as ever." She gave me the stank face, "it's because I'm pregnant again Kamaya," she told me while rubbing her stomach. "Oh shit my bad well congratulations. I guess your still good for something. Anywho let me get out of here, y'all have a good one."

I ended up getting something to eat after talking to dumb and dumber and as I was sitting there minding my business this guy comes over and tries to sit down and have a conversation like I wanted to be bothered. "Excuse me miss lady, I noticed you when you over there getting your food so I just had to come over and say hello and see if maybe we can exchange numbers," he said to me. Looking him up and down I noticed a couple of things that weren't attractive at all. First of all his teeth looked nasty, his clothes looked a little too big, like he had on one of those long ass tees dudes used to wear in the 90's. I'm looking at him like son don't nobody wear them shits anymore. His whole aura was just bad so I had to turn him all the way down. Standing up so I can get away from him I said "I'm good luv, enjoy," and just walked away. "Fuck ya fat ass then stuck up bitch!" I'm not sure why dudes have to get so nasty when you turn them down. Just take the L on go on about your business. I didn't even respond to his ass. I had to get home to get ready.

Arriving home I noticed Tyson wasn't there so I figured he just went to the store or something so I decided to just go get myself together for the party. When I stepped out of the shower into the bedroom I saw that he came back and was already dressed. "Hey baby give me like 20 minutes I'll be ready to go," I told him while drying off. "Uh Kam I think I'm just gonna go ahead and go without you." I looked at this fool like he as crazy. "Tyson I know you didn't invite me out just to damn uninvite me at the last damn minute." "Kamaya I just need some time to myself so maybe we can do something tomorrow or something." This nigga is really tripping right now with this bullshit. How you gonna say you need time to yourself but your going to a whole damn party. This was a question that needed an answer.

"Tyson how the fuck are you going to say you need time to yourself but your going to a party with people so you won't be by yourself asshole!" "Yeah I know that Kam, I'm just saying I want to go out by myself and just enjoy my peoples. I don't want to have to deal with making sure your comfortable and all that other shit." "Nigga fuck you, fuck ya friends, and fuck that bullshit ass party!" After I said that he just turned around and left out the door. This is the bullshit I don't like with him, he does shit like that and then acts like I'm crazy for tripping.

See he doesn't realize that he already told me where the party was so I was going to let him get comfortable and be having the time of his life then I was going to pull up on his ass. Let me call Gabi and see if she's going to roll out with me. "Bitch I need you to lace up ya sneakers and meet me at my house in 15 minutes." "Aight I got you," she said and hung up the phone. See that's the thing about her, she's always ready to roll regardless. I'll fill her in on what's going on once we are on our way. I threw on some sweats and some sneakers, put my hair in a bun and went outside to wait for Gabi.

"So where are we going and who are we finna roll up on?" Gabi asked as soon as she walked up to my porch. "Tyson's bitch ass, he invited me to a party and as soon as I'm getting ready he suddenly decides he doesn't want me to go. Talking about he wants to go alone because he doesn't want to worry about making me comfortable and some other bullshit. All fucking lies if you ask me, so bitch I'm pulling up to see what's really going on!" I was heated because this nigga was really trying to play me like some sucka. More than likely he got a bitch there or something so that's why he told me he didn't want to go. We drove about 30 minutes before we got to the place where the party.

I pulled up right next to his car and imagine my surprise when I see him and three other chicks sitting in the car smoking. He really got me fucked if he think it was cool to leave me home but he can be chilling with three bitches like he single. I walked right up to his door and snatched it open. "Nigga you must think I'm stupid!" I punched his ass right in the damn face. The girls just got out of the car and was standing there just looking. "Damn Kam what you hit me for?" He had the nerve to ask me like what he was doing wasn't wrong. "Nigga you out here in your car with three bitches while you left my ass at home, how the fuck you think that look?" "Ma it wasn't like that, this is my cousin and her friends, all we were doing was smoking nothing else." He tried to convince me it was nothing but to be honest I didn't believe him.

"To be real with you Tyson I don't believe you and quite frankly I don't give a fuck what was going on. You on some real sneaky shit and I'm not beat for it. You tried to convince me you needed time for yourself but you out here caking with other chicks, so tell me if the shit was the other way around how would you feel about it." "Kamaya don't play with me like that, you wouldn't do me like that would you?" See that's the problem with these dudes they can do whatever the hell they want to you but the minute you do the same thing it's the end of the world. I looked at him and just smirked, "maybe I will one day," and I turned around to get back in my car. The chicks must have went back inside the party or somewhere, I don't know and could care less. Them hoes didn't owe me shit so I wasn't sweating them. Before I got in the car all the way Tyson grabbed my arm and turned me towards him. "Kam baby, it wasn't nothing like that but I apologize if I made you feel uncomfortable." "Whatever Tyson maybe I'll see you at home, maybe I won't." I left him thinking I may not go home for the night and pulled out of the parking lot.

On the way back to my house Gabi and I talked about what just happened and of course she didn't fully believe him and hell I didn't either but I don't know for a fact what it was so I was just going to keep my eyes on him. I hugged Gabi goodbye and went in the house to take a shower. I locked my room door, Tyson wasn't bringing his ass in here tonight, he better sleep on the couch or go find those bitches he was with earlier. That incident was weighing heavy on my mind and couldn't go to sleep right away. I've already been played by two other dudes, is this one going to be the same way. I tossed and turned for a little bit and once I finally fell asleep here comes Tyson banging on the door.

"Kamaya please let me in baby, I told you I was sorry even though I didn't do anything wrong." This is the problem with him and pretty much every dude out there, they always think they didn't do anything wrong when they do. "Actually Tyson you did do something wrong, your out chilling with other females knowing you got a girlfriend who was supposed to be with you and more than likely them chicks didn't even know I existed. They looked like they were surprised I pulled up on you." "Nah baby they know I got a girl, shit everyone knows, they probably was just surprised you punched me like that." I wasn't convinced and I was tired of talking to him so I told him to go think about what happened while he slept on the couch. I said goodnight and took my ass to sleep. He tried knocking on the door a couple more times but I ignored him and he finally got the hint and walked away.

TWENTY-SEVEN

THE NEXT MORNING I woke up to see Tyson staring at me with a tray of food. You're probably wondering how he is in here if I locked his ass out of the room. Well I'll tell you how, his crazy ass picked the lock. "Good morning Kamaya" he said smiling at me and he leaned in to kiss me but I turned my head. "How the fuck did you get in here?" I asked him while I was eyeing that tray of food. I'm always hungry and that food sho was smelling good. "I picked the lock, how you think I got in." He said that shit like it was a normal thing to do. "I mean I would have done it last night but I figured I'd give you some space." Well how nice of you I sarcastically responded to him.

"Like I told you last night Kamaya I'm sorry for what happened but you have to believe me, nothing was going on. The one chick is really my cousin, the other two girls were just her friends. They weren't checking for me and I wasn't checking for them. My cousin asked me if I wanted to smoke with them so I did. Nothing more, nothing less. I promise you I won't make you question my loyalty to you again." I'm probably stupid for believing this but he was so convincing and honestly he wasn't doing anything but sitting there and smoking. It's not like I caught him fucking another bitch but either way the shit was questionable.

I told him I'll forgive him this time but he better not let no shit like this happen again. Of course he reassured me it won't but who knows. After we finished talking he fed me the food he made. It was pretty good, he made some pancakes, eggs, bacon and he cut up some fruit for me. Sometimes he makes some really good food and some other times not so much but I don't know how to tell him because he thinks he's a real chef.

So after I finish eating we sat there and just continued to talk. He was rubbing my feet and his hand just kept going further and further up my leg until he reached my pussy and he started rubbing on my clit. It didn't take long for me to get wet. "Damn ma ya shit wet already" It didn't take much for me to get wet and since he was rubbing on me like that it was damn near impossible for me not to get wet. One thing that bothers me about Tyson is he doesn't eat pussy. Well tonight he tried and I can see why he doesn't. It was like a cat drinking milk from a bowl. I had to teach him how to do it and after a few minutes he got the hang of it and it was good enough to make me come at least once. Once I came all over his beard he came up and put his dick in me so slowly it was like he was trying to tease me. Slowly going in and out of me he whispered in my ear "I'm sorry Kam, I love you so much and I don't want to hurt you." "Shit Tyson I love you too," and I came for the second time all over his dick. He began pumping faster and he came a few minutes after I did. For the rest of the day we just stayed in bed.

Neither one of us had anything to do today so we just stayed in bed all day. We would eat, fuck, sleep, watch tv and repeat. He was off for the night so it was nice just being able to spend time like that. Even though we made up since the incident last night I still had this nagging feeling in the back of my mind. It was like something was telling me that there was more to that story but since I couldn't prove anything I decided to wait and see how things play out. They always say what happens in the dark comes to the light.

While Tyson was sleep I noticed his phone kept ringing and it was the same 770 area code. Now I know he had family in Georgia so maybe it was one of them. At first I tried to wake him up but he would not get up for nothing. After the person called a couple of times and left a message they decided to text him instead. Imagine my thoughts when I read the text message that said, "hey baby I miss you and I can't wait for you to come back." So I'm looking at the phone surprised as hell and now I'm starting to put two and two together. Every couple of months Tyson goes to Georgia, he claims it's to see his family but I'm starting to think it's to see this bitch that's texting him. It seems like everything is going wrong in this relationship. The minute we get past one thing something else happens.

I tried to see how many times they have called or texted each other but I couldn't unlock his phone. So I decided just to wake his up. I tossed the phone right on his chest just as it started ringing again. "Who the fuck is this bitch texting you from Georgia talking about she can't wait for you to come back!" I screamed at him when he finally woke up. At first he looked like he didn't know what I was talking about but then he noticed the person was calling his phone.

He just kindly pressed ignore and looked at me with the most sincere face he come up with. "Kam this is nobody, I've had this number for a long time so anybody can be calling. You're the only girl I'm with and the only girl I'm worrying about. You know how these chicks be, they see you happy and they want to try and break things up. I'm not thinking about nobody else but Kamaya Jones and that's my word."

Did I believe what he was saying? Hell no but at the same time it was one of those situations where there wasn't 100 percent proof. Just because a bitch was sending text messages wasn't a guarantee that it was legit. I love Tyson but my guard is definitely up with him. I think part of the problem is I'm not sure if I want to start over with anyone else and I don't even know how to. Tyson was a very good liar, it was to the point that you can know he was lying but for some reason it seemed like he was telling the truth. He had my mind gone and he was so manipulative that he made you think you that you were the one in the wrong. Let's just say this was another incident that Tyson pretty much got away with.

A couple of weeks go by and things have been pretty good with Tyson. I'm still watching his ass because to be honest I don't trust him anymore. The problem is when things get too good, Tyson seems to not like it and he finds a way to start an argument or something. I think he enjoys chaos in his life. The minute I think we are finally having a good thing going he comes and fucks it all up. There is always a complaint about something. Like today he's bitching because Gucci was barking while he was sleeping and I get it. Your trying to sleep because you've been working and the dog woke you up but there was no need to be starting an argument with me. Sometimes when he gets like that I just leave his ass alone. The headache and the arguments are worth it.

Today I decided to take Summer to the park to have some mommy and me time. We took Gucci with us too so that way crybaby Tyson can get some sleep. He gets on my nerves a lot but I do love him and I think he loves me and he always finds a way to convince me that things are going to get better and they do but only temporarily.

My grandmother was sick so I tried to spend as much time as I could with her. Summer and Gucci always made her feel better so I took them both with me. We sat with her for a while and she told me something that surprised me. She said "Kam baby that Tyson isn't the one for you so sooner or later baby your gonna have to let him go." I just sat there because I've been feeling the same way too and I was surprised because she always seemed like she liked him. "I know your probably surprised by what I just said but I felt the need to tell you. Now don't get me wrong he's a nice young fella but just not for you." She continued to tell me her feelings about him and she prayed that I found the happiness I deserved. She knew about all the other things I went through with Quran and Jamil and she didn't want me to get her again by Tyson. I just sat and listened to everything she said and I ensured her that I would be good. We stayed for a few more hours and it was nice seeing her happy with Summer and Gucci. Who would have known this would have been the last time I saw her alive.

TWENTY-EIGHT

LATELY I'VE BEEN FEELING like Tyson is bipolar or something. It's like one minute he's up then the next he's down. And it's not regular up and down, it's like he's either super excited or super down. There is no in between for him. He'll be so excited about doing something then within minutes, sometimes seconds he becomes sad. It's weird to witness sometimes. At times I feel like I have to walk on eggshells in my own house. Things have definitely been changing between us but he doesn't see it.

In the morning when I get dressed for work I tend to do so in the dark and I try to be as quiet as possible. One day I dropped something and it woke him up so he began yelling at me. I didn't pay his ass any mind. Sometimes an argument isn't worth it. The crazy part is he'll wake up later and not know what happened or he pretends not to know, so he's confused as to why I be having an attitude.

He still has the tendency to invite me places but then at the last minute changes his mind but of course he still goes. As usual when I say something about it he gets an attitude then he'll leave. Sometimes he gets so mad that he just ups and drives to GA no matter what time of day or night it is. This further makes me think that he's messing with someone there. Now I get you may miss your family but if you were going to keep going back and forth so much you should just stay there with them. I mean shit I would. That's too much money and time to keep going back and forth like that.

It's like I try not to even be to happy with him anymore because the minute it's going good he finds a way to fuck it up. I know it's just a matter of time before we have some sort of fight again and he'll probably end up driving to Georgia again. I just don't get why he's even still here. It seems like he's not happy sometimes but when I try to end things he tries to find a way to make me stay. Honestly it's like I'm just a convenience to him. I guess he just needed to stay with me so he doesn't have to go back to his moms house.

Hearing his keys in the door I prepared myself for whatever attitude I was going to get today. "What's up ma?" He asked as he walked over to me and kissed me on my cheek. He sat down and put my feet on his lap and started rubbing them. All I can think in my mind is what is he up to. Lately it seems when he's extra nice to me he wants something. Maybe today will be different.

"How was your day baby?" He asked me still rubbing my feet. "It was pretty good, got some cleaning done, read a little and just relaxed.

I needed it, I've been so busy with trying to get my practice together and stuff. And of course the baby keeps me busy. I took her and Gucci to go see grandma the other day and that made her happy. How was yours?" I asked him. "Mine was good, but I need a small favor if possible." See I knew he wanted something. He wasn't one of those people who did something nice just to do it, it was always a motive behind it. Giving him the side eye I asked him what he needed.

"Okay Kam so hear me out." I already knew it was about to be some bullshit. When a dude says hear me out he's usually about to spit some dumb shit, but I'll give him the benefit of the doubt. "So listen right, I saw this car I want to buy and I'll fix it up then I'm gonna sell it for double the price. Whatever I make off it I'll give you half." This fool must be crazy I thought to myself but I was gonna see exactly how much he was trying to get. "Okay and how much money are you asking for?" "I only need about $800 and I probably can get like $1600-2000 for it once I clean it and stuff. I promise Kam I'll give you the money back."

"Oh you mean like the money you were supposed to give me the money back from the check you stole from me!"

"Damn why you have to bring that up Kam? I told you I was gonna give you the money back and I will if I can flip this car." I'm sitting here thinking to myself this fool must think I'm stupid. Why the hell would I give him more money and he already owes me money. No sir, I'm not doing it. "Listen Tyson I get what your trying to do but I don't have it and to be honest even if I did I wouldn't give it to you anyway," I told him. "Oh so it's like that Kamaya, that's how you doing your man?" I can tell he's getting mad because he called me by whole name and he only does that when he's mad.

"Yes Tyson that's exactly how I'm doing it, I can't just be giving money out for unsure things. I have too much shit going on to be just throwing money away. Sorry but I can't do it." "You know what fuck you Kamaya!" he yelled at me. "Yous a shellfish ass bitch" I was looking down so when he called me a selfish bitch my head popped up so fast I thought the shit was going to break. "Me, selfish," I asked him while pointing at my chest. "Mutha fucka I'm far from selfish. I let you move in here, you barely help with the bills, you drive my car, I have purchased multiple things for you, and you stole from me and I didn't press charges but you call me selfish!" I know he's bugging right now to think I'm selfish in any way. I could have gotten his ass locked up just based off him stealing from me, and if you add everything else I did for his ass I'm far from damn selfish.

"Yes Kamaya you are selfish, I just needed a little help from you and you can't even do that and you wonder why I don't be taking you nowhere with me. Because of shit like that." I'm not sure what one has to do with the other, they didn't really, and it made no sense. "What does one have to do with the other Tyson? I tell you absolutely fucking nothing! Your just trying to find a bullshit excuse as to why you do the shit you do. Well let me tell you, there is no fucking excuse Tyson for the shit you do! With that I walked out the damn house. I didn't feel like arguing with his ass.

TWENTY-NINE

AFTER I CAME BACK LATER on that night Tyson tried to act like nothing happened. He has a habit of doing that. We never actually try to fix our issues because as soon as I try to talk about it he shuts me down and never wants to talk me about it. Lately I've been feeling like this relationship isn't going to work but then he does something nice that makes me rethink things. Like today I was sitting at home relaxing before I went to run some errands, and my doorbell rang. I wasn't expecting anyone so I wasn't sure who it could be.

When I opened the door there was a guy standing there with some flowers, a teddy bear and some chocolate candy. "Hello are you Kamaya Jones?" He asked me. "Yes I am" I said smiling at him. He was kinda cute. No harm in flirting. "Well miss these are for you" He said handing me the stuff. "Thank you" I told him and closed the door. I had no business trying to flirt with the flower shop guy while I'm still in this situation. I went to put the flowers in some water and noticed it had a card in it.

Reading the card it said "Kamaya I'm sorry for the way I've been acting lately and I really love you and I promise to make things right." While this was a nice gesture I wasn't really feeling it. It's like how many times is he going to keep fucking up and apologizing just to do some dumb shit all over again. At this point I was pretty much over his ass. I don't even feel the same anymore. Every other day there was some type of problem. He'll do something, apologize just to turn around and do something else. It's like a never ending cycle and I'm over it.

My phone rung snapping me out of my thoughts. I answered the phone and it was Tyson's ass. "What's up ma, did you get the flowers I sent you?" "Yes Tyson I got them and they are beautiful. Thank you" "Anything for my favorite girl," he said trying to sound sweet. I really didn't think his voice was cute or sweet anymore, honestly at this point it was getting on my nerves. I think that he thinks it's sexy but you can tell he's trying too hard. I'm tempted to just hang up on his ass. "So Kam besides the flowers I got you and ya girls a spa day today. I just want to prove to you that I'm sorry and I'm going to do better." I rolled my eyes but trust me I was definitely going to take this spa day and make sure Gabi and Keysha came with me. "Thank you Tyson, I appreciate it." Anything for you baby, I love you and enjoy your day he said to me before hanging up.

. . .

Welp let me let the girls know to get ready for our spa day. I guess the errands I was going to run after to wait until later or another day. Let me get up and go get ready. Grabbing my phone I sent a group message out.

Me: Get ready y'all like soon, sorry ass Tyson is sending us on a spa day.

Gabi: Yass bitch you know I'm down and it's on his dime, count me in

Keysha: I'm down.

Me: Cool, I'll see y'all in about a half hour.

I decided to just throw on a Pink sweatsuit and some Nike slides. I figured I have to be comfortable and wear some shoes that were easy to take off. While I was getting ready to walk out the door my phone rung. When I looked at the screen I couldn't believe it was Jamil calling me. It must be trouble in paradise on his end. Well isn't this a pleasant surprise I said answering the phone. "Hey Kam, how are you?" He asked me still sounding sexy as hell. I'm good J, how are you? "I'm doing okay but I was calling because I wanted to see if maybe we can go have lunch or dinner sometime soon." For a second I didn't know what to say, like should I or should I not go with him. It didn't take me long to decide. Sure I'll go with you, I told him. "Fa sho well how about tomorrow at 12, meet me at the DoubleTree downtown, they have a restaurant in there that has a good lunch menu." I told him that was cool and we talked for a couple more minutes before I had to hang up and get my ass out of the house before Gabi and Keysha start calling me fussing.

. . .

A few minutes later I ended up at the spa and of course they both beat me there. When I walked in they both just started laughing. "I'm not even going to say anything Kam," Gabi said to me shaking her head. "Well there is a reason why I'm late and I'm not even that late." Mhmm go on, Keysha said. "Sooo as I was getting ready to leave the house, Jamil called me talking about having lunch or dinner and I ended up talking to him on the phone for a little bit and that's why I'm late."

"And what was your response to the date?" Keysha asked me.

"I told him yeah and we are meeting at the DoubleTree for lunch tomorrow."

"So let me get this straight Kam you agreed to go to lunch at a hotel with a man you were in love with for years and honestly I don't think you're completely over him," said Gabi. It always had to be her to point some shit out that I didn't want to think about. Did I really still love Jamil, actually I did even though I moved on with Tyson. Hell Tyson didn't treat me half as good as J did even though he was married.

"Y'all are making a big deal out of nothing. It's just an innocent meal between two friends nothing else." I tried to reassure them but I think I was more so trying to convince myself. What if it did mean more, nah it probably doesn't I mean he's still married and I'm not trying to go down that road again and I'm in a relationship so nothing is happening. They both looked at each other and started laughing.

"Who does this bitch think she's fooling, they'll be downstairs eating and next thing you know he has her in one of those rooms upstairs banging her back out." Gabi said and kind of loud too. I assured them nothing was going to happen and I changed the subject. We continued to enjoy our spa day and it was very relaxing. I didn't tell them but I was looking forward to this lunch date with Jamil.

. . .

The next day came and I was actually starting to feel a little nervous about this lunch. What if he wanted more, hell what if he wasn't married anymore and wanted to try again. What would I do, I mean I know I'm getting tired of Tyson but was I completely ready to leave him. The answer should be yeah but who knows. I may be over-thinking this whole thing. He could honestly just be wanting to have a friendly lunch. Let me get out of my thoughts and get myself together.

I decided to wear a black pencil skirt and a blue crop top. Just because I was plus size didn't mean I couldn't wear crop tops. I'm not sloppy fat so they looked good on me. I slid my feet into some blue flip flops, grabbed my little black clutch and was out the door. I had to make sure I looked good.

Arriving at the hotel I double checked my Mac lip gloss and headed inside. I didn't see Jamil so I went over to sit at the bar. I ordered a mimosa since it was still early in the day. After waiting about 10 minutes, he smelled him before I saw him. He always wore Issey Miyake and I loved it. I wonder if he wore it just for me or he just never changed. "Miss Kamaya Jones," he said to me while grabbing me out of the seat. "Mr. Jamil Smith," I said while hugging and secretly inhaling his cologne. I had to suppress a moan when he hugged me, he smelt so good and it felt good being in his arms for that quick moment. He held me for a few minutes before he finally let me go. "Damn Kam you looking good as hell, I mean you always looked good but today you look extra good." He said to me while licking his lips.

. . .

I can't believe after all this time I still get butterflies around him. I should be over him after all this time especially because I have a boyfriend but unfortunately I'm not. Maybe if Tyson treated me better I wouldn't still be feeling like this over J. My throat suddenly got dry and I had to take a sip of my drink. Clearing my throat I told him how he looked good too. He even had the beard shining. We ended up getting a table and while we ate we had basic conversations about what was going on in our lives. We sat there for a couple of hours and had a couple of drinks even though it was the middle of the afternoon. Next thing I know we were in one of the suites and he had me pinned up against the wall with my skirt around my waist.

THIRTY

"DAMN KAM I missed you so much," Jamil said while kissing on my neck. That shit was feeling so good too but in my mind I'm saying this is all wrong but my body was screaming it's all right. I really did miss with J, shit I'll be lucky if I get any foreplay from Tyson so I was definitely enjoying this. "Hmm J we can't do this," I moaned out to him when his hands slid my panties to the side.

"Kam I need you just one more time, these couple of years have been rough without you." I don't even know what to say to him especially because he's rubbing the hell out of my clit and I'm on the verge of cumming. "I feel it Kam just let it go," he whispered in my ear and I did on his command. It's crazy how he can still control my orgasm.

After my breathing returned to normal he carried me over to the bed and just as he did before he proceeded to suck the soul out of me. I came again two more times before he decided to put it in. We went at it a few times before we both passed out.

The sound of my phone ringing jarred me out of my sleep and I noticed it was my mom. "Hi mom," and as soon as she called my name I knew something was wrong. "She's gone Kam" and I immediately broke down with her. She was calling to tell me that my grandma had died. Granted she was 94 years old and lived a good life but it still didn't make it easy. I tried to calm my mom down and after I knew she would be okay for a little bit I hung up the phone.

My crying must've woke Jamil up because he just grabbed me and rubbed my back and told me everything was gonna be okay even though he didn't know what was going on. I just laid there and cried my eyes out for a good half hour before I got myself together to tell him what was going on. "J my grandma just died," I said crying all over again. "I'm sorry baby," was all he said. I mean honestly what do you say to someone when a loved one dies. He just continued to hold me and let me cry until I couldn't cry anymore.

I felt bad because I'm sure he had to get home but he told me he wasn't leaving until he knew I was going to be okay. I finally decided to let him go and I stayed at the hotel for a while longer and went back to sleep. A couple of hours later my ringing phone woke me up and when I realized what time it was I figured Tyson was probably worried about where I was.

"Kam where the fuck are you!" he screamed in my ear as soon as I answered the phone." First of all lower your damn voice," I told him. "Tyson my grandma died today and I needed some time to myself I'll be home in a little bit," I said to him and hung up the phone. I wasn't in the mood to deal with his tantrums. I got up, freshened up, and headed home. I noticed J had texted me so I responded to him and ensured him I was going to be okay and I thanked him for everything.

When I got home Tyson was sitting in the living room watching tv. As soon as he saw me he jumped. "Kam baby I'm sorry for tripping on you earlier, I was just so worried about you." "Whatever Tyson, listen right now I just want to take a nice hot bath and go to bed. It's been a really long day and I have a headache so I just want to go to sleep." I guess he was feeling guilty about yelling at me because he came into the bathroom and washed me from head to toe.

"Bae I'm really sorry about your grandma and I'm sorry I yelled at you like that. I'm so used to you coming home at a certain time and when you didn't come I started to get worried. I shouldn't have yelled at you like that." "Your right Tyson you shouldn't have but you did and honestly it doesn't even matter anymore. I'm just ready for bed." After rinsing off in the shower I put on my pajamas and got in the bed. Tyson came in after me and held me. "I really love you Kamaya and I'm always going to be here for you." He told me, but I didn't even respond. I laid there and cried myself to sleep. I couldn't believe my little g lady was gone.

The next day I woke feeling a little better so I called up my girls to go have lunch. We decided to meet at Applebee's, then we were going to go shopping. I needed something to distract me. I really didn't want to drive so I asked Gabi can she pick me. After getting myself together I heard her beeping the horn. When I went outside Keysha was in the car with Gabi. I couldn't wait to tell them about what happened with Jamil but I'll wait until we get to the restaurant and get a drink first.

"Kam I'm sorry about your grandma, she was like a grandma to me to" said Keysha. "She was a grandma to all of us" Gabi co-signed. "Thanks, her funeral will be this Friday." I informed them. "So let me tell y'all about what happened with Jamil." I proceeded to tell them everything from our dinner, to the hotel, and how Tyson spazzed out on me. "Girl I told you he was gonna have you face down, ass up," Gabi said a little too loud for my liking. "Y'all I really missed him but us messing around can't happen again. He has a wife and even though I barely like him, I still have a boyfriend. I refuse to play second again for him or anyone else. "You deserve so much better than him and Tyson's crazy ass," said Gabi. We proceeded to catch up on everything that's been going on our lives and I needed this break. My girls always know how to cheer me up.

Today was one of the worse days of my life. It was time to say the final goodbye to my grandma and it really hit me that she was gone. I thought the day couldn't get any worse but boy was I wrong. In usual Tyson form he found a way to mess up my day. It all started when I first woke up. He started nice by making me breakfast, but one thing I noticed was that he likes being nice to me when he wants something or when he's about to fuck up my day. Now I know he can't be that insensitive to ask me for anything on this day of all days.

I handled my hygiene then I went into the kitchen. "Good morning Kam, have a seat I made you breakfast," he walked over to me and kissed me on the cheek and even pulled the chair out for me. I looked at him sideyed because he was being extra nice but I definitely wasn't going to turn down this breakfast. There was eggs, pancakes, bacon, and some tea. I told him thank you and proceeded to eat. I had a feeling the bullshit was coming because when he sat down he cleared his throat.

"So Kam I know today is an important and sad day but I won't be able to go the funeral with you." I dropped my fork on the plate and just stared at him for a good ten seconds before I responded. In my head I counted to ten to try and calm myself down. I know he's been selfish lately but to not be there for my grandmother's funeral was beyond selfish to me. I was still just sitting there astounded that he can be so cruel.

"So let me get this straight, YOU, I said pointing at him, YOU my boyfriend has decided at the last minute to not to attend my grandmother's funeral with me. You know she was one of the most important people in the world to me and you can't be there to support me." At this point I had tears running down my face. "Seriously Tyson

what is so important that you can't be there for me today of all days?"
"Kam I have to go somewhere with my brother, plus you weren't
there for me when my grandmother died." It was at this moment that
I realized that not only was he selfish but he was dumb ass hell.
"NIGGA I DIDN'T KNOW WHEN YOUR GRANDMA
DIED!" I couldn't believe he said that shit, like his grandma died
before I even met him so how the fuck would I be there for him if I
didn't know his ass existed. He's really out of his mind.

"It's whatever Kam, either way I'm not going." Of course he said
it's whatever because he really didn't have a comeback to what I just
said. "Tyson you know what FUCK YOU!" For me this was the last
straw. I was tired of arguing with him, I was tired of his selfishness, I
was just tired of it all. I walked out of the kitchen and went to go get
myself ready. I didn't have the energy to go back and forth with him.
Today was for me. I've already been through enough shit and i refuse
to keep putting myself through anymore.

After I got myself together I left the house to head to the funeral.
I drove myself because I needed some time to myself. I really had to
get rid of Tyson's inconsiderate ass but right now I had to focus on
getting through this service. My girls came through for me like they
always do. Even Quran and Tati came and I think I saw Jamil there
too. After the service we had a small repass at the church. My
grandma was so well liked by a lot of people so all day people kept
coming up to me offering their condolences. As I was sitting there
eating I noticed Quran and Tati heading to me. "Kam I'm so sorry
about your grandma, she was like a grandma to me too while we were
growing up." That was one thing about Tati, she was a hoe for what
she did but she was always there for my grandma and I appreciated
her for that. "Thank you Tati and thank you for always being there
for her even through all the shit we went through." I surprised myself
when I got up and hugged her. That will probably be the last time
that happens but we all were there for a bigger cause and I decided to
be a bigger person.

After everyone left, I headed to pick my baby up from Quran's moms house. I just wanted to get in bed and cuddle with my baby. I had a lot of thinking to do and I know it was the end for me and Tyson. There is no way I can be with him after today, Now the only thing is how to get rid of him and making sure he doesn't sucker me into staying with him. It was time for me to put Kamaya Jones first.

THIRTY-ONE

SO WITH ALL THIS crazy shit going on with Tyson I finally decided to call it quits after a couple of years. What took so long? Who the hell knows, that was one manipulating bastard. Every time I thought I was going to leave he found a way of convincing me he was going to change. Each time it was something different. All the apologies meant nothing at this point, not the flowers, cards, candy, none of that shit. I finally had enough and it was time to finally let him go.

There was nothing he can do to convince me to stay anymore. Today I was going to meet him in a neutral place to break things off with him. Hopefully I can make this quick and easy.

Arriving at the diner I got a little nervous. Sometimes Tyson has a bad temper and I'm praying he doesn't cause a scene in this place. I sat in my car for a few minutes to get my thoughts together. Walking inside I noticed he was already there and he was sitting there like he didn't have a care in the world. Once he noticed me he got to greet me and he pulled out my chair for me. Oh now this nigga wants to be a gentleman I thought to myself. "Hey sweetheart how are you doing today?" Why is he pretending like his selfish ass really gives a damn about how I'm doing. "I'm good Tyson, how are you?" "I'm better now that I see you but why did you ask me to come here?" He looked at me so intensely I got a little nervous. Clearing my throat I said, "Tyson I love you and care about you but I can't be with you anymore. Things between us have changed and I just can't deal with it." While I'm talking to him I notice this little twitch in his eye and you can tell he's about to start getting angry.

"What do you mean Kamaya that you can't be with me anymore?" He asked me like he didn't understand what I meant. "Tyson I mean me and you can't be together." "I heard what you said but I don't understand where this is coming from." I'm sitting here with my head tilted to the side like a puppy because I know he is not acting like he was this great person all along. "Tyson let's be real here, you've lied, stolen, and probably cheated on me. Your attitude changed and I don't know the person you are now. You are a totally different from the person I met a couple of years ago." "Of course I've changed Kam, that's life, people change." You changed for the worse not the best, I told him. "You have lied to me countless times, you've manipulated me, hell you even stolen from me which was definitely something you didn't have to do."

He grabbed both of my hands and looked me in both of my eyes while talking to me. "Kam listen to me like I've told you before there is no leaving me. I'm good to you girl, I've never beat on you and I never brought no diseases home. I'm a good dude, I could have cheated but I didn't.

"Oh wow Tyson, there are other things that make you a not so good boyfriend. Just because you didn't beat on me and haven't given me any diseases doesn't mean you never cheated on me. Everyone that cheats doesn't get a disease. Even if you weren't cheating you damn sure gave me reason to think that you were. You would invite me out to places then right before it was time to go you would suddenly say I can't go. It's like you were trying not to get caught by someone or you just didn't want to be seen with me."

"Nah Kam it wasn't like that it was just sometimes I wanted to be by myself. Me going out was the only way I was able to do that sometimes. I was never ashamed of being with you Kamaya, you are a beautiful ass woman inside and outside. I'm sorry if I didn't appreciate you the way I should have and I wouldn't ever make you feel like that again. I'm for real this time."

I sat here and looked at him like he was crazy. This fool thinks I was going to fall for this shit again. Well actually I can see why he thought that because I have fallen for it more than once so yeah I can see it. "No Tyson" I said looking at him directly in the eyes. "Hear me and hear me clear, what we had is over and I wish you the best." With that I got my ass up and walked out of there. I wasn't trying to go back and forth with his delusional ass. As I was walking away he grabbed my wrist and said "Fuck you fat bitch!" "Oh I got ya fat bitch you mediocre ass dick nigga." I picked up my drink from the table and threw that shit right in his face then I punched him the damn face. The fuck he thought this was. Calling me a fat bitch didn't faze me because shit I am fat but the disrespect wasn't necessary. Fuck his ol boring dick ass.

I felt so much better walking up out of there. It was like a weight was lifted off my shoulders and I felt so much freer and lighter. I decided to just take a stroll for a little bit to enjoy my new found freedom. As I was walking I thought about what Tyson said about never leaving me and me never leaving him. I have this feeling that this won't be the last I hear from him. It's crazy how now he decides to say something about my weight but all this time he acted liked it never bothered him. I'm not worried about the shit though, I'm perfectly fine with my weight.

Continuing on with my walk and just enjoying my peacefulness, I thought I saw a familiar face but I just knew it couldn't be who I thought it was. There was no way I just saw Khai fine ass all the way in New Jersey. My eyes had to be deceiving me but I sure was about to go find out. I walked down to the coffee shop and I thought I saw him go in but after I looked everywhere for a minute I didn't see him. I actually got disappointed even though I wasn't sure if that was him in the first place. Since I was here I decided on getting some coffee and a muffin. It was my turn to order but before I even got a chance to I heard this deep voice right behind me.

"Just put whatever she's having with mine," he said and when I turned around let's just say I didn't realize that I was holding my breath. Just the feel of his breath on my neck sent chills up my spine. I even smelled the mint gum he was chewing. "Hello Kamaya long time no see, it's been a couple of years right?" He asked while smiling at me and I swear this man looks even better than he did before. I instantly got turned on which is all the way wrong, I mean shit I just broke up with Tyson not even five minutes ago and already thinking about another man's dick. I started singing Mariah Lynn's song, once upon a time not long ago I was a hoe! Laughing to myself I noticed Khai just standing there staring at me. "Oh I'm sorry Khai, I must have zoned out. Hi how are you?" He reached in to hug me and baby when I say I never smelt a man smell so good in my life. I think I inhaled extra hard.

"What are you doing here in New Jersey? I asked him. "Well I just relocated here with my job. One day I'm in Miami next thing I know I'm in New Jersey, who knows where I'll end up next.

Depending on what happens here maybe I'll just stay here," he said while winking his eye at me. This man was doing something to me that I wasn't familiar with. Everything about him oozed sexiness and I found myself getting butterflies in my stomach just by looking at him and smelling him.

"What are you doing here miss lady?" "Oh I live here and have been all my life. Miami was just a little vacation for me." "That's cool, maybe you can show me around sometime since I don't know anybody else here. I can use a friend and who knows what else can happen between us." Damn he sure was laying on the charm but I had to snap out of the daze his ass had me in. It was way too soon to entertain someone else no matter how fine he was. I'm sorry Khai but I'm going to have to decline. I'm just in a place right now where I can't even deal with men in the friend capacity, so with that being said thank you for the coffee and muffin but I have to go. Enjoy your day and goodbye. When I stood up to leave he grabbed my hand and looked me right in my eyes and said, "don't make this a goodbye Kamaya because I will definitely be seeing you around again, I can promise you that." I just smiled at him and left. If I stayed there any longer I would have gave into anything he said and if he wanted he probably could get me bent over his couch by the end of the night. It's time to focus on Kamaya and get my shit together. I'm so close on opening my practice so that is my focus right now. Maybe me and him would cross paths and who knows what will happen.

THIRTY-TWO

THE LAST FEW weeks have flew by. I'm close to opening my practice soon so that's something to be excited about. I haven't had any issues out of Tyson or anybody else for that matter. I can say my life was pretty peaceful. The only thing is I kind of wish I would have gave Khai my phone number. I haven't seen him since that day but I guess that was a good thing. I'm officially on a man strike. These niggas out here don't know how to act. Let me call my girls up and see if they want to hit the mall with me. I need a new outfit for the grand opening. Well not really but hell ain't no such thing as too many clothes. After talking to them for a few minutes we decided to meet up at the mall.

I walked around for a little bit before I found them. "Hey my bitches!" I guess I was too loud because this lady next to us looked at me all weird. I just gave her the side eye and went on about my business. "So anyway before I was interrupted by miss miserable face, what's up with y'all?" "Nothing much girl," Keysha spoke first, "but honey let me tell you Tyson has been going through it since y'all broke up. He keeps talking about how sorry he is and how he wants you back. He knows he made a mistake and he'll do anything to fix it. Girl I get tired of listening to his ass, whenever he comes over I leave or just go into the other room. That shit is aggravating," she said while rolling her eyes.

"Well his ass should have thought of that before he did all the shit he did. You can't keep doing shit and expect someone to forgive you each time. I know I should have left him way before I did, but since I didn't I think he finds it hard to believe that I actually left him. He acts like he was boyfriend of the year or something. Maybe worse boyfriend of the year but definitely not the best. Enough about him guess who I ran into?" They both looked at me like I was crazy. "Bitch don't nobody have time to be playing guessing games, who did you see?" Gabi always had to be extra, like why couldn't she just say who or guess I thought to myself.

"Anyway, remember that dude I said I met in Miami that J was trying to fight. Well I ran into his fine ass at the coffee shop a couple of weeks ago and he looks even better than he did before. He tried to get my number to be his friend and show him around the town since he's new here. Apparently he just moved here and doesn't know anybody here but I couldn't give him my number. I need to stay my ass away from men, especially bearded men I said to them laughing but I was dead ass serious. Them bearded niggas been nothing but headaches to me so I'm good."

"So you mean to tell me you let that fine ass man get away again. It must be some type of fate for him to end up in Jersey and so close to you. It's crazy how out of all the coffee shops in this town y'all end up in the same one. You really don't think that's a sign Kam?" Keysha questioned. Keysha always thought that things were signs or fate and maybe in this case she was right but I'm too afraid of letting anybody else get close to me. I'm tired of being hurt. "Yes Keysha you are probably right but I don't think I can take another heartbreak and I feel like Khai can possibly be the one to break my heart." Now it was Gabi's time to talk, "listen Kam you can't let a couple of fuck boys make you give up on love for the rest of your life. Now I'm not saying Khai will be the love of your life but you will never know if you don't give anyone else a chance honey."

"I get what your saying Gab, hell both of y'all but I think I need more time before I can think about someone else. Y'all know I have to focus on getting this practice open and I also want to start a website and a online blog. I think it may benefit other women who may have experienced some of the same things I have. You never know who your story may influence one day, I want it to be called Kam's Corner. I can pretty much discuss anything from outfit of the day, books, love, anything us women like to talk about. It would have different themes and have a question area where people can ask me different things or make a suggestion about my next blog. So for now that's what I'm going to be focusing on."

"We understand honey and we are with you all the way but we just want you to be happy. If nobody deserves it Kamaya, you do. You are the kindest person I know and someone will come along and prove to you that there are still good people in the world besides us." We all laughed and hugged and continued on our shopping trip. After we had dinner we all decided to go our separate ways. As I was walking to my car I had this eerie feeling like someone was behind me but every time I turned around no one was there. I hauled ass to my car because I didn't like the feeling. Getting in my car I put on Jungle by H.E.R, this song was my shit. I turned the radio all the way up and peeled out of the parking lot hoping to shake that feeling. After a few minutes I noticed this car that seemed to be following me. Every time I changed lanes they changed lanes. I have no idea who it could be but I hightailed my ass straight to the police station. I was not about to get caught slipping and get killed out here plus I forgot my gun at home. Once I turned into the police station the car kept going. I waited for like twenty minutes before I decided to leave and continue heading home.

Once I arrived home and went inside I double and triple checked all my door and windows. I was wondering who the hell could have been following me. I haven't heard from Tyson in a while so I doubt it's him. The only other person I know that had any beef with me was Jamil's wife and I haven't dealt with him in years so I highly doubt it's her either. So at this point I have no clue who the hell it could be. I was going to call Gabi and Keysha and tell them what happened but before I got a chance to my phone started ringing. I looked at the caller ID and it was Tyson. I'm surprised he called me, I was debating on answering or not. He called about three more times back to back so after the fourth time I finally decided to answer.

"Hello Tyson how are you?" "Hey baby girl I'm good, listen Kam I know you said what we had was done but I can't let you go that easy baby. I need you in my life and I'm really sorry for everything I've done to you, you have to believe me. I will never hurt you again baby, I love you girl." He sounded like he was on the verge of crying but I wasn't about to fall for that shit. Let me try to explain it to him again. "Listen Tyson like I said before we can't do this. You messed this up and there is nothing you can say to change my mind. I wish you all the best in the world and one day someone will make you happy but that someone isn't me." He sat there completely silent for about twenty seconds so I knew an outburst was more than likely coming.

"Bitch I told ya fat ass before you ain't leaving me! Right now we are on a break, you'll be back soon. I was the best thing that happened to you." Is this nigga on some type of drugs or something? Did he really think he was that great of a man. I just sat here silently laughing at his ass while he continued on his rant. "Ya fat ass better think twice about trying to play me. Your ungrateful as hell and don't appreciate shit when people are trying to do nice things for you. I promise you if you leave me I will blow up your car and steal that damn dog you love so fucking much. If you don't come to your senses Kam your gonna lose out on me." Bitch when he said that I looked at my phone cause he clearly was tripping. I decided I heard enough and just hung up the phone on his ass. He attempted to call me back to back multiple times until I eventually just turned my phone on do not disturb and took my ass to sleep. I had a long ass day and I really needed to sleep.

About three o'clock in the morning I heard this noise in my house. For a minute I just layed there thinking maybe if I'm quite enough they will go away thinking nobody is home. Even Gucci didn't bark, his little ass not that tough. After a while it got quiet again so I attempted to go back to sleep but this time with my gun by my bed. Once I finally got back to sleep I hear someone say Kaboom bitch! before everything went black.

THIRTY-THREE

WHEN I FINALLY WOKE UP I was inside some type of warehouse, tied up to a chair. I'm not sure how the hell I got here or even who brought me here. I don't even know how long I've been here. All I remember is someone coming into my room saying kaboom or some shit and I was out. The voice didn't even sound familiar. I haven't done anything to anybody so who the hell would want to cause harm to me. The only person I can think of is Tyson but I don't think he would go that far. Well shit maybe he would considering he threat-ened to steal my damn dog and blow up my car so maybe anything is possible.

I looked around the room to try to see if there were any clues as to where I'm at or anything that may be a hint as to who kidnapped my ass. Suddenly I started laughing, like who the fuck kidnapps a whole damn adult and I ain't no skinny bitch either so whoever did it must be strong as hell or had some damn help. I think I laughed for about five minutes to the point of tears coming out of my eyes. At first my tears were laughing tears than they turned into tears of fear. What if whoever it was is going to try and kill me and nobody will find my body. Shit what about my baby, who's going to take care of her if I'm gone. I was on the verge of having a panic attack. Breathe bitch breathe I had to tell myself while taking deep breaths. After I got my breathing under control I thought I heard something like a door being unlocked. Maybe someone was coming to save me. That hope was short lived once I saw who was coming in. Well, well, well look who's awake.

I couldn't believe my eyes well then again maybe I could. It had to be Tyson's crazy ass to kidnap me but why. Like I know he's not tripping that hard over me breaking up with him. "So Ms. Kamaya I know you're probably wondering why your tied up to a chair and not sleep in your comfy bed with your precious little dog. By the way the little shit bit me but I spared his life so you better be grateful I didn't kill his little ass." He's really acting like the shit he is doing is normal. No sir adult kidnapping is not normal. Shit kidnapping period isn't normal. "Tyson why are you doing this? What we had was good but I can't do this with you anymore and for you to kidnap me is taking things way too far. You do know I have a baby to get back to right?" "Yeah I know that Kam and I also know she's with her dad for a few days so she'll be good and it gives you enough time to come to your senses and take me back." He said the shit with so much conviction like it was really going to happen.

I have to find a way out of here because this fool is really crazy and I don't know if he will kill me or not. I decided to keep trying to have a conversation with him and try to convince him to let me go. I don't think he realized it but I'm not tied as tight to this chair like he thinks I am. As he was talking I was slowly loosening up the rope and planning the right time to try and escape. I really don't think he planned this whole thing through. There is literally a bat sitting a couple of feet from me so once I get loose I can grab that and popped his ass right in the head with it and hopefully get the fuck up out of here. "Kam I'm not in the business of begging anybody for anything but for you I'm willing to make an exception." He acts like I want him to beg me for anything. All I want is for him to let me go so I can use the bathroom and eat. Shit I'm hungry.

"Tyson if you untie me we can talk about us getting back together." I can see the glimmer of hope in his eyes but it didn't last long because maybe he knew my ass was lying. "Bitch you must think I'm stupid! You trying to get me to let you lose so you can leave." "No I'm serious we can talk about starting over but right now I'm very uncomfortable and i'm hungry and really really have to use the bathroom. Just let me use the bathroom and get me something to eat and I promise we can talk." I started to feel confident because he looked like he was going to do it but then he suddenly turned to walk away. "I'm going to go get you something to eat but when I come back we can talk about this relationship." Shit little did he know there will be no discussion of a non existent relationship but for now I was going to play along. While he was gone I took the opportunity to loosen up the rope a little bit more and eventually get myself lose.

I started to smell food and I knew Tyson was back so I had to pretend like I wasn't plotting my escape. "Kam baby I'm back," he yelled out. "I got you some food and I think I'll feed it to you then we can talk. I want to show you that I can be romantic like you want me to be." Did he really think it was romantic to be feeding me while I'm sitting here tied to a chair and I still have to damn pee. I'll admit the food was good but I was ready to go! I still don't know how long I've been here. "Uh Tyson, how long have you had me here?" "Oh it's only been a day Kam." "Damn it feels like it's been longer than that but I do know that I'm ready to go now." I kindly told him. "Before I let you go Kam, I need to know that we will be together." "Yes Tyson we can be back together," and as soon as he started coming to me, I loosened my hand and when he got close enough I punched him right in his face, jumped out the chair and grabbed the bat.

"Bitch did ya fat ass just hit me?" See that's the thing with him, he acts like really cares for me and loves me but when he gets mad and things don't go his way he gets to name calling and being down-right disrespectful. "Yes the fuck I did and if you think about coming near me I will pop ya ass with this bat." I guess he thought I was playing because he tried to lunge at me and I bopped his ass right in the back with the bat. "I told you not to come any closer and you did anyway," I said while hitting him multiple times across his back. Once he fell to the ground I hauled ass up out there. Running outside I realized I wasn't that far from a store so I ran inside to call Gabi or Keysha so someone can come pick me. I probably should call Keysha since she's the calm one. Of course she didn't answer the phone so I had no choice in calling Gabi. "Gabi come get me, Tyson crazy ass kidnapped me!"

I stayed inside the store waiting for Gabi. I just told the store owner I was waiting for my friend to pick me up. I didn't want to tell him what happened because there was no need to get the police involved. Tyson's bitch ass was going to get his sooner or later. For right now I just need to get home and change my locks and shit. About 20 minutes later Gabi showed up so I hauled ass out of that store.

"So bitch what you mean Tyson kidnapped you!" She didn't even give me a chance to get in the car before she started asking questions. "Yes exactly what I said, Tyson broke in my house and kidnapped my ass. Like who the fuck does that! I was literally in my bed sleep and I heard a noise but thought nothing of it at first. Wait let me rewind and tell you from the beginning. You know I broke up with him and he called me fat bitch, threw the drink in his face and shit. Well later on that day I kept feeling like someone was following me but I never saw anybody. I go home, everything is locked up and shit. So Gucci and I are in bed sleep and like I said I heard a noise but it didn't alarm me. I eventually fell asleep and sometime during the night I hear someone say "kaboom bitch" and the next thing I know I wake up in a warehouse tied to a damn chair.

Gabi just sat there and looked at me like she was in disbelief, I mean I guess she was because I would have been too. "So he goes on and on about us being together and shit. Talking about he's going to do better and be romantic and just saying shit he thinks I want to hear. His ass didn't even have me tied up that damn tight so when I got a chance I got loose beat his ass with something and got the fuck up out of there and here we are." "Damn Kam I can't believe his crazy ass did that shit, like dude we broke up get the fuck over it. So what are you going to do now? You know Keysha is going to feel bad since she hooked you up with him." "I know she is but this is definitely not her fault. Hell she didn't know he was that crazy. Matter of fact call her up and see where she's at." After we got ahold of Keysha we went over to her house so I could tell her what happened.

"Omg Kamaya I'm so sorry this happened and I feel like if I didn't hook you up with him none of this crazy shit would have happened to you." Keysha sincerely said to me. "Aww honey it's not your fault, you didn't know he was batshit crazy and if I would have seen him in the streets I still may have talked to him and the same shit would have happened, so please honey don't blame yourself." After we sat there and talked about some other stuff and reassuring Keysha none of this was her fault, Gabrielle and I left so I could go home and get my locks and shit changed. Maybe I need to get a new gun too, because the next time someone tries some shit like that again they may end up getting shot.

THIRTY-FOUR

THESE LAST FEW weeks have been crazy. I'm finally two days away from opening my own practice and I couldn't be more excited. A couple of times I had dreams about Tyson kidnapping me but so far I haven't seen or heard from him. I think at this point I'm giving up on love, these niggas out here ain't shit and I don't need to get my feelings played with and my heart broken again. There's a chance the next mutha fucka that screws me over may end up dead.

I had to move on from the shit and keep my life going the way it was supposed to. I can't say that it was easy or even going to be easy for a while. Tyson really scared me. I feel like I'll never be able to trust anyone ever in life. He would lie about the dumbest things so I think that everybody else will lie about everything too. I started to feel insecure about myself as well. Like what is it about me that makes these dudes want to cheat on me or lie to me about things. Was I that bad or did I just have a bad habit of picking up the wrong guys. I can't be the only chick out that these things happen to but damn like the only three dudes I've been with shitted on me. I know none of their asses would tell me if it was me so I was just going to try and do some soul searching and see what I come up with.

My daughter and my business were the most important things to me right now so I had to focus on those two. If love was meant for me then one day I'll get it. I just hope I'm not too afraid to let someone in. The way I feel right now I think it's going to be impossible. In the words of Omarion, "I got this ice box where my heart used to be." The words to that song were so true. My heart turned cold from all the fuck shit that went on. No need to dwell on it though.

I got asked out on a few dates but I turned all of them down. I was too afraid to start something new with anyone else. All these dudes were the same, they all lie and all are full of shit. I haven't had sex in a while but my bullet did the trick. I can't be out here just doing it to anybody. If or when I become interested in some else I'm going to take my time before I get into another relationship.

Tyson not contacting me was short lived because he ended up calling me and when I didn't say what he wanted to hear he got nasty with me. He called me all types of names, told me I was weird, and antisocial. I think his ass really didn't know what those words even meant. It was crazy how when I answered the phone he was nice but soon as he realized I wasn't buying into his shit he got real angry and started yelling and shit and I would just hang up the phone. This would go on at least once a week. I would block him then he would find another number to call from and I had to block each one of those numbers too. It's like he wasn't going to give up.

One person that I haven't seen in a while is Khai. I'm not sure if he is still in town or we just haven't crossed paths lately. Maybe it's a good thing that I haven't seen him because now that I'm single I may end up giving him my number but I don't want to end up in the same boat again. Then again if I did see him he may not even be interested in me anymore, hell he might have found one of these chicks out here. That could be another reason why I haven't seen him.

Today was finally the big day. The grand opening of my own practice. So far it's just me but I have a few counselors, a couple medical assistants, and a receptionist. I was so excited that I barely could sleep the night before. I worked hard for this and my hard work is finally going to pay off. A Better Way was my baby and I hope it ends up being something good for the community. Not only was I going to be taking appointments in the office but I was also going to do online counseling if they wanted to. In another year or so I want to open up a shelter but I want it to be one side for women and children and another side for men. I want to make sure everyone is safe and I know sometimes women don't want to be housed with men. I also want to be able to provide job training as well as help them find housing. There's not enough help in black communities so I'm going to try to do everything in my power to change that. Like the saying goes, be the change that you want to see.

When I arrived at the building I noticed it was a big turnout. Even the mayor came out. I wasn't surprised though because he was heavily involved in the community especially things that will help improve the community. Everybody showed up for me and I was getting teary eyed just seeing all the support I was receiving. Some of my college professors as well as classmates were there. The doctor I was under when I did my internship at the hospital was there. Of course my girl were there, as well as Quran and Tati. Even Jamil showed up. Thank goodness he left his wife home because lord knows she probably would have acted a fool and today is not the day for that.

Once I cut the ribbon I gave a speech. "I just want to say thank you to everyone for coming out and to everyone who helped me out with this dream of mine. Whether you helped build the building, offered words of encouragement or even just showing up today, I greatly appreciate each and everyone of you. This office is so important to me because there isn't enough awareness and help in the African-American communities in regards to mental health and my team and I would like to kickstart that change. Once again, thank you for coming and make sure to tell a friend to tell a friend. Now come in and look around, we have some snacks and drinks. Feel free to pick up any information or make an appointment with my receptionist Michelle, and just enjoy yourselves.

As soon as we all got inside Gabi and Keysha came over to me hugging me. "Girl we are so proud of you." "Thank you and y'all know I went through so much trying to get this thing together but no matter what I was not letting anybody stop me from doing this. It's been my dream and I really appreciate y'all for being there for me through it all. I really do love and appreciate y'all two." By this time I started crying even though I was trying not to. I could never show Keysha and Gabi how much I appreciate them. They have stuck by me through everything and not once have either one of them judged me and for that I will be forever grateful to them.

I continued to make my around the room. I noticed Tatianna at the desk talking to Michelle, I wonder if she was making an appointment for herself or just getting some information. I didn't have to wonder for long because her and Quran were heading my way. Quran spoke to me first. "Baby mama I just want to tell you how proud I am of you," he said then hugged me. "Kamaya I know things would never be the same with us but I know how this has been a lifelong dream of yours and I'm very happy and proud of you. I hope we can at least be cordial towards each other and maybe we can do some type of counseling to move on." I was surprised she was saying all this and to be honest I forgave Tati a long time ago. I had to forgive her and Q in order to move on with my life. By all means we would never be friends like we were but we had to have some type of dealings with each other since our children are siblings. By the way her ass looks pregnant again. Pretty soon they will have their own football team. I agreed to go to counseling with her for the kids sake. Since our situation wasn't too drastic at this point, I was going to set up a couple of sessions with one of the counselors. I talked to them a little bit longer and then proceeded to make my way around the room again. I felt someone grab my arm and when I turned around I was surprised by the person in front of me. "I told you baby there was no escaping me," he said while grabbing my wrist really tight.

THIRTY-FIVE

I COULDN'T BELIEVE Tyson was really here right now. It seems like he gets off on trying to make my life hell. Instead of bothering me he needs to be taking some pamphlets and making an appointment because clearly he has some type of problem. "Tyson why are you here harassing me? You should really make an appointment to see one of the counselors here," I said to him while trying to get my arm loose from his tight ass grip.

"Kamaya I told you I was never letting you go and I meant that shit ma. You are everything to me and I love you. I just want to support you and make you happy." This fool must really think I'm stupid to believe the bullshit that's coming out of his mouth. During this whole process he was barely there for me so I know he's full of it. I started to think that he was intimated by what I was trying to do with my life. What he didn't understand about me was if I rocked with you, I rocked with you and I try to make sure everyone in my life is taken care of and I try to push everyone to reach their full potential, Tyson included.

"Tyson please don't come here with that. You weren't really supportive of any of this. You would complain about the hours I was putting in trying to get all this together. Everything was good when things were going your way but the minute I did or said something you didn't like you would curse me out and give me your ass to kiss. Oh and let's not get started on how you bailed on me for my grandma's funeral. Ooh and how about the late night calls from that girl, whatever her name was. Let's not forget the constant running back and forth to Georgia, probably to see that same girl. Think about all the shit you did to me and really ask yourself would I still want to be with you." He was still holding on to my wrist and I noticed his jaw starting to twitch which means he was close to going off and I was praying that he didn't cause a scene here.

"I was good to you Kamaya and you know that shit," he was starting to get loud so I had to find a way to calm him down before people started to notice what was going on. Before I could even respond to him I heard a voice that I haven't heard in awhile but was very familiar with. "Hello Kamaya, I had to make sure I came and spoke to you and congratulate you on your practice." Just the sound of his voice was turning me on even under these circumstances. "Hi Khai, how are you? Thank you for coming." I noticed how he kept looking between me and Tyson and I think he figured out that something was going on that shouldn't been.

"Say Kam is everything okay?" Khai asked me. "Yeah my man she good!" Tyson said before I could answer Khai. "Bruh I wasn't talking to you, I was talking to miss Kamaya. So Kamaya is everything okay?" he asked again. "My dude there is no need to be asking my girl anything" and I looked at Tyson like he lost his damn mind. There is no way in hell he can sit here and claim me as his girlfriend. "Tyson don't sit here and lie, you know damn well me and you aren't together anymore so don't be saying that." "Oh so that's how you want to play things Kam?" "Tyson I'm not playing about anything, you and I broke up months ago."

By now people were starting to notice what was happening so I had to hurry up and try to defuse the situation. "Listen Tyson please don't do this here. I will call you later and we can talk, okay?" "You got that Kam but make sure you call me," he said finally letting my wrist go and kissed me on my cheek. He told Khai he better watch his back then he left.

"Damn Miss Kam, this the second time I saw you and you had some dude going crazy. I was going to ask you on a date but I'm scared now, you might have me out here going crazy," he said to me chuckling. When he did all I could do is look at how damn sexy his smile was. His teeth were so white and perfectly straight, I couldn't help but to stare at them. "Well Mr... that doesn't happen all the time but if you did ask I would have to decline your offer." I gave him a gentle smile.

"I'm hurt," he said with his hand over his heart. "I just don't think now would be a good time to give you my number." See I need time to get myself all the way together and with Tyson lurking around I don't think it's a good idea to try to deal with anyone right now in any type of capacity. I can see myself actually liking Khai and I don't think I'm ready for that.

"I understand but do you think we could at least be friends?" "To be honest Khai, you probably would be a good friend but right now I don't think I even need friends. Maybe one day, I just can't today." He was about to make this hard for me the way he was looking at me. I can't do it though. I'm sure as much as we keep running into each other I'll see him again, hopefully he's still single.

"Trust me Miss Kamaya I'll see you again and I'm going to keep trying. Once again congratulations on your practice and you enjoy the rest of the night." He kissed me on my cheek and walked away. Damn even his walk was sexy.

"Where the hell was y'all bitches a few minutes ago when Tyson was all in my damn face? I asked Gabi and Keysha as soon as they walked their asses over to me. I didn't even realize these broads left me all alone with psycho ass Tyson. This fool really was crazy and I better watch my back because I have a feeling he'll be coming back around again. I probably should have gotten him arrested when he called himself kidnapping me.

"Kam I swear we were on our way over here but then we seen that dude come to your rescue, so we stayed back to watch everything play out." Gabi told me. "Girl that was Khai's fine ass and Tyson tried to act like we were still together or something. For a minute I thought they were going to fight but thank God they didn't. I didn't need that type of mess going on here. Anyway, Khai was trying to get my phone number but I don't think I'm ready to deal with anyone else not even in a friend capacity."

"Honey trust we understand and you should definitely take your time before you deal with someone else. You've been through enough to go through anymore crap." Keysha told me. "Y'all are definitely right and I'm gonna make sure the next one if there is another one, that they aren't married, or bat shit crazy." I told them. We continued to talk for a little longer and I noticed people starting to leave so I made my way around the room to thank everyone again and say goodbye to them all.

After locking up I went home to take me a nice relaxing bath. Today has been a long day and besides the crap that Tyson pulled it was a good turn out. My team and I have appointments for the next couple of weeks and we were working on setting up our website to do online counseling as well.

I lit some candles and put some music on and sat thinking about everything in the last few years. Listening to *Love Don't Play Fair by Sammie*, I thought about everything I went through from Quran cheating on me with my best friend. Jamil having a wife and keeping it a secret and Tyson's psychotic mess, I'm not sure if I'll ever be ready to deal with someone else. I'm a hopeless romantic though so there is still a small part of me that has hope on finding love.

THIRTY-SIX

LATELY I'VE BEEN TRYING to get myself into loving myself again. Those past relationships put me through so much and sometimes I feel like I lost some of myself as well as not loving myself like I should. I'm following this author Asia Monique and she has her group doing a self love journey where every week she poses a question and a task for us to complete. We should keep a journal of our journey. Week one was "What do I think about me?" This was an interesting question and one that took me a minute to think about. I thought I was smart, pretty, funny, a dope chick, but I also felt scared, broken, insecure, and unsure. When you deal with multiple men and they break your heart it's normal to feel insecure because it makes you wonder what did you do wrong for them to treat you like that. I'm also afraid of moving on and unsure of how I will even be able to allow someone in again.

My girls have always been there for me and they always offer words of encouragement and they even try to convince me to start dating again but I don't know about that. If and when I decide to date again maybe I will give Khai a chance if he's still available. I've had a few opportunities since Tyson and I broke up but none of the guys were really interesting to me. I'm gonna have to be very careful about who I date next.

Tonight me and my girls were going out since we never officially celebrated my practice opening. Plus after the last few weeks I had I needed to go out and have some fun. We were going to our usual spot. It's not like it's too many places out here to go to anyway, so club Fetish was the place to meet on Friday and Saturday's. Tonight I chose to wear a red bodycon dress with some black Une Plume Sling wedge heels that I treated myself to. I added some gold accessories with my Ruby Woo lipstick and I was all set to go. We were going to meet up there so I grabbed my keys and was out the door.

When I pulled up I noticed it was packed and it was going to be hard to find a parking spot but I got lucky when I saw this car backing out of a spot. I hurried up and pulled in before someone else got it and luckily it was kind of close to the door. Lord knows I didn't want to walk too far. Gabi and Keysha were waiting for me by the door so we all can walk into together.

Walking in they were playing Knuck if you Buck, it don't matter how old that song is it still goes hard. That is definitely one of the songs I get ratchet to so we headed to the dance floor first then we were going to go to our VIP section we rented out for the night. They played a few more old school songs so we stayed out there for a little bit. Making our way to the section multiple dudes were trying to talk to us but I wasn't interested. I was to busy trying to get to the section to sit down and get something to drink so I kept it moving.

The waitress came over and she had a bottle of Louis XIII that we clearly didn't order. "Um excuse me we didn't order this bottle," I said to the waitress. "Yes I know you didn't, the gentleman over there sent it," she said as she pointed to the other vip section and when we looked over Khai was sitting there holding his cup and he winked at me. I just nodded my head and mouthed thank you.

Turning back around Gabi and Keysha were both looking at me all crazy. "What y'all looking at?" "Bitch you must have busted it open for him to send that expensive ass liquor over," Gabi damn near screamed. "First of all keep it down and no I didn't do anything. He asked me for my number at the grand opening but I turned him down. I haven't seen him since that night." I was wondering myself why he sent such an expensive bottle.

I guess I don't have to wonder for too much longer because he was making his way over here. "Hello ladies," he said to us smiling. "Hi," we all managed to say at the same time. "Khai thank you for the bottle, you didn't have to do that," I said to him. "It was no big deal plus I wanted to say congratulations again for opening your practice, so look at it as a celebratory bottle," he said while licking his lips. I'm not gonna lie when he did that I had to clinch my thighs together. I can admit Khai is a fine ass man but the way my heart is set up I can't mess with him.

"Well thank you again, how about taking a couple of shots with us, you can invite your boys over too." I figured we might as well chill with them. Khai waved his friends over and when they came I noticed how Gabi was looking at one and he was looking at her the same way. I admit they both were fine as hell. The other one was looking at Keysha but she wasn't paying him no mind, she's still with the security dude.

We both did the introductions and I found out his friends were name Bane and Chris. Bane was the one that had his eye on Gabi so he went straight over to talk to her and Chris went to talk to Keysha . Of course Khai and sat next to me. "So Miss Kamaya, how are you, what have you been up to?" I told him about how busy my practice was and basically that's it. He told me about his week and he was chilling for the weekend with his friends since they weren't from here.

We all just partied and chilled for the next few hours. All three of the guys were really cool and it seemed like Bane and Gabi really hit it off. Khai walked me to my car while the guys walked the girls to their car. "Kamaya are you going to give me your number this time?" "Um I'm gonna have to decline again," "Damn," he said to me while wiping his eyes pretending to cry. "Miss Kamaya you have hurt my feelings once again but I won't give up." "I'm sorry Khai, it's not you it's just that I'm not ready yet." I told him. "I got you ma but like I said, I won't give up," then he kissed me on my forehead and helped me get into my car.

I did enjoy his company tonight but am I really ready to start something new with someone. Nah not yet but I will keep him in mind when I am ready. I drove home thinking about Khai. Everything about him said he was a cool dude but hell the last three were until they weren't. Only time will tell. Since he said he wasn't giving up I'm sure I'll see him again.

Making it home a few minutes later I realized I was more tired than I thought. I managed to take a quick shower and got in the bed, after I let Gucci out for a few minutes. Once my head hit the pillow I was out. Unfortunately my sleep didn't last too long because I kept hearing a dog bark which in turn made Gucci bark. Getting up to see what was going on I heard a noise in my backyard. When I turned on the backlight imagine my surprise to see Tyson creeping around my damn yard.

THIRTY-SEVEN

"TYSON what the hell are you doing creeping around my yard?" I screamed at him but not too loud because I didn't want to wake up my neighbors. "Kamaya baby I just wanted to talk to you, that's it." He was talking like it was normal to be creeping around in someone's yard. "Well most people will call before they come, or knock or ring a doorbell instead of creeping around in the yard. What if I would have shot you? "Kamaya you wouldn't have shot me because you love me too much." I started laughing in his face, I mean I laughed so hard I had tears coming out of my eyes. This fool must be on some type of drugs or something to think I still loved him.

"Kam listen just give me like 5 minutes to talk to you and I'll leave you alone."

"Tyson you got 5 seconds to get out of my yard or I will call the police."

"You know what Kamaya fuck you, that's why you are going to be a miserable lonely bitch!" He screamed at me. See this exactly why I don't deal with him in any capacity. The minute I say something he doesn't like he spazzes out on me.

"That's fine Tyson, have a good night." He proceeded to leave my yard and I went back in the house and made sure all the windows and the door was locked. Shit it's not like he hasn't broken into my house before. It was going to take me a while to go back to sleep because I'm afraid he may come back but if he does again I'm killing him.

After tossing and turning for a while I went back to sleep and managed to get a few hours of sleep. I was going to meet up with Gabi and Keysha for breakfast before I went into work since my appointments were later today. I didn't feel like really getting dressed today so I just put on some pants, a blazer, and some flats. I didn't have the energy for heels. Once I got the baby ready for daycare I headed out the door.

We decided on meeting up at IHOP so I dropped the baby off then headed over there. Of course they beat me there since I'm always late. When I walked in they were already at a table. "Good morning ladies," I said to them while walking up to the table. Gabrielle started looking around all crazy so I was thinking someone was behind me or something. "Um Gabi why the hell are you looking around like that?"

. . .

"Because Kamaya I'm looking for Summer Reign where is she?" She asked me.

"Chile I dropped her off at daycare already. It was easier for me to drop her off before I came here since I'm closer to my office from there. Anyway what's going on with yall?"

Gabi spoke up first, "well Bane and I exchanged numbers and we are going to go out before he goes back home."

"Oh that's nice, Gab, I hope you have a good time and don't do nothing I wouldn't do," Keysha said. "Which means don't do anything," I laughed. Keysha was definitely the most innocent one out of us three. I think we kind of balanced each other. Gabi was the most free spirited one, Keysha was more quiet and reserved and I was somewhere in between. It made things fun and interesting with us. I knew no matter where we were and what was going on we were going to have a good time.

After eating and chatting with them I left to head to work. Today I had a pretty busy schedule so hopefully my day will go by fast. It was exciting and interesting doing what I do but sometimes it was draining. It was hard listening and trying to help people with their problems when I had problems of my own. That's why it was important for me to talk to a counselor every couple of weeks. I can't keep everything bottled up and expect to help others.

When I got to the office I was surprised to see Jamil sitting in the waiting room. I don't remember seeing his name on my list so I'm not sure what he was doing here. "Good morning Jamil," I spoke to him. "Good morning Kamaya, do you have a moment so we can talk?" He asked. I wondered what he had to say because we haven't really talked in a while except the night of the opening. "Sure follow me to my office," I told him. "So what's up, what are you doing here?" I asked him. "Kam first of all let me just apologize again for everything that happened between us. I just wanted you to know that I really did love you, hell I still do. You made me see things in myself that I never seen before and for that I am forever grateful to you for that. Also I'm here because my wife and I would like to try marriage counseling and I know this is the place to come." I was surprised that he would come here of all places for that considering this is my practice but truth is I had some of the best therapist and counselors in the area. I hope he doesn't think I'm going to be helping them, that would be pushing it. "Wow, well that's good for you guys, you don't expect me to counsel you guys do you?" He chuckled, "oh nah, I just wanted to let you know and again apologize for everything. Don't worry I will try to schedule our sessions around your schedule so you don't have to see us." Well I appreciate that and good luck to you both. Take care J." "Thank you Kamaya and you take care as well." After that he left. I sat down in my chair and thought about what if J wasn't married, would things have worked between us or not. I mean he treated me well and I really believed he loved me but he has a wife so we will never find out. If he got a divorce I'm not going to lie if I'm still single I would attempt a real relationship with him. Then again it may not be a good idea because if he cheated on her who's to say he wouldn't cheat on me. Oh well let me stop thinking about shit that won't be happening.

The morning flew by pretty fast and when I looked at the time I realized it was time for lunch. Since I had a nice size breakfast I decided to go to the little deli around the corner from my office. It was nice outside so I decided to walk. When I got the there I ordered a half of a turkey and cheese sandwich and some broccoli cheddar soup. The soup was so good but sometimes it didn't agree with my stomach but I'll deal with that if it happens. After I got my food I decided to sit at one of the tables by the window so I can people watch. I noticed a familiar face walk past and come into the deli. Maybe he won't notice me. That was short lived because when he got his food and looked for a table he spotted me.

The closer he got to me I smelled his cologne and damn did it smell good. He was looking good today, well he did everytime I saw him. He had on a black suit with a peach colored shirt that looked good against his skin. It also looked like he just got a fresh haircut. Mhmm there is something about a man in a suit with a fresh shape up. For a minute I stopped eating just to watch him walk over here.

"Is this seat taken?" his deep voice asked me. Before I got a chance to answer he already put his tray on the table and was pulling out the chair. "No its not taken." I told him.

"Well do you mind if I sat with you?" I told him I didn't mind so he sat down directly across from me. "I'm starting to think your stalking me Khai, first the coffee shop and now here."

He laughed, "nah I'm not stalking, my office is right across the street so I come here pretty often," he said. "Oh okay, what office do you work in over there?" "I'm a senior accountant at Johnson and associates accounting firm." I must say I was impressed by that because you don't see too many young black accountants and at the senior level at that. He has to be really good with numbers. Maybe I'll use his services one day because I suck at all of that shit.

"That's what's up, I may need your services one day," I told him.

"No problem, just let me know when your ready," he said handing me his business card. We sat there eating and talking for the next hour. I found out the company was his father's and soon he would be taking it over and that was why he ended up moving here. It was nice talking to him and this time he didn't even ask for my phone number. Even though I probably still wouldn't have given it to him yet anyway. "Well Khai I have to get back to my office, it was nice talking to you and I'm sure I'll be seeing you again since the food is so good here. Enjoy the rest of your day." "You do the same Kamaya." With that I got up and left. Damn if I didn't have a client coming I probably would have tried to stay and talk to him all day.

THIRTY-EIGHT

THE LAST COUPLE of weeks have been going pretty good. I've been bringing my lunch so I haven't been back to the deli which means I haven't run into Khai again even though I would like to. I saw Jamil and his wife a couple of times when they came in but nothing crazy happened. I guess his wife realized she got him and is keeping him so there is no need to continue to fight with me. Luckily for the most part they come when I'm not there or I must already be in my office.

I'm still keeping up with my self love journey and it's been helping. This week we had to write five things that we were thankful for. To be honest it took me a minute to think about it because sometimes we aren't thankful for simple things that we should be thankful for. For instance I'm thankful for having peace in my life and my home, because lord knows when Tyson was around my life was everything but peaceful. It was a lot of chaos and now I'm starting to really enjoy my peace of mind. Of course I'm thankful for my family and friends. Also I'm thankful for my health and my career. I also share all my journal questions and entries on my blog. Hopefully it can help someone else. There is also a task each week and this week it's doing something nice for someone so I think I'm going to volunteer at the homeless shelter.

Today I had a late day so I decided to catch up on some reading, today I was reading *Fallon and Wali by Saja Jay*, this book was so good it was hard to put it down. I have read every book she has written and I have not been disappointed. The ringing of my phone snapped me out of my thoughts. When I looked at it I saw it was Tyson so I sent his ass right to voicemail. I don't know what the hell he is calling me for. I know he don't want shit. He never does. Luckily he didn't call back because sometimes he'll call until I answer. A minute later a text message came through. When I checked it it was a picture from Tyson and it was of him and some girl. See this is the shit I'm talking about. Who does shit like that. Then he'll be mad when I block his ass and that's just what I did.

I put my phone on DND just in case he decided to try and call me from a different phone number and I really wanted to finish this book. Today I had plans with Gabi and Keysha. We were going to go bowling and catch up. I wanted to know what happened with Gabi and fine ass Bane. Khai, Bane and the other guy whose name I forgot was all fine ass hell. Summer was with her father, apparently they wanted to take the kids to Chuck E Cheese or somewhere. I heard that Tati was pregnant again, I done lost track of how many kids they got now. Like I said before better her than me. Anyway I ended up finishing the book and got up to get dressed.

Since we were going bowling I just put on some jeans with a burgundy shirt and some burgundy converses and put my hair up in a messy bun. I decided to catch a Lyft because I didn't feel like driving plus there's a chance I may have a few drinks and I don't want to risk driving home. After waiting ten minutes for my Lyft they notified me they were outside so I grabbed my Gucci fanny pack and headed out the door. This fanny pack definitely came in handy.

A few minutes later I arrived at Lucky Strike and looked for the girls, looking around I spotted Keysha but not Gabi so she must not be here. I stopped at the counter to get my bowling shoes and headed over to her. "Hey Keysha, how long have you been here?" I said while hugging her.

"Oh I just got here a few minutes ago and I came over here to secure a lane for us," she said hugging me back. "Oh okay, I guess Gabi will be here soon." As soon as I said that I saw Gabi coming through the door.

"You gotta be kidding me! Kamaya Jones actually got somewhere before me and on time at that," she said while walking towards us. "Whatever hoe I could be on time sometimes," we all looked at each other and laughed because I'm almost never on time. We waited for Gabi to get some bowling shoes so we can start. I can be competitive sometimes so I was really trying to beat both of them.

We played a few rounds and we each one won a round. Afterwards we went over to the bar to get something to eat and have a couple of drinks and catch up. This joint had some of the best burgers so all three of us got a burger and a frozen margarita. "So Gab how was your date with Bane?" Keysha asked her. "Girl that date was everything and then some. We went and played mini golf, then we went to Mccormicks and Schmidt's for dinner, you know I love some steak and seafood. We went for a walk by the lake and ended up in his hotel room," she said while twerking in her seat.

"So what happened when y'all went back to his room?" I asked her. "Honeyyy lets just say he did things to my body that I didn't know was capable of being done."

"You had sex with him on the first date?" Keysha questioned. Sometimes Keysha can be so naive but its not in a bad way. "Yes I sure did, hell it's not like he was going to be here that long and it was so much sexual tension between us I figured why not. Shoot I gotta get it when I can and there was no way I was letting his fine ass go without testing the waters honey." I totally agreed with her, shoot as long as they both are single, agreed to it and protected themselves then why not. That's what's wrong with people now, they are so set on what people may say about them that they limit themselves to certain things in life.

"I'm happy you enjoyed yourself and you deserved it. Will y'all be seeing each other again whenever he comes back or do you plan on going there sometimes?" I asked.

"Yeah we talked about it but I don't know when, with the way our schedules are it might be hard."

"Oh Kam I forgot to tell you that Tyson came by with some girl the other day but asked about you when the girl went to the bathroom. The crazy thing is she seems to really like him but its clear he's still stuck on you." Keysha told me.

. . .

"I know about the girl because his dumb ass gonna send me a picture of him and her and when I didn't respond he tried to call me but I didn't answer and put him right on the block list. I guess he call himself making me jealous. I'll be glad when he realizes that I don't want anything to do with him anymore. He tries to call me like every damn week. When I do answer he is either too damn nice or too damn mean, there is no in between with him and I don't have time for it."

I wasn't about to sit here and talk about Tyson and ruin my night so I quickly changed the subject. We sat there and talked for a little longer then we went to bowl some more. After I hit a strike I was walking back to sit down and I heard someone say "hey fat bitch, I see Jamil dumped ya fat ass!" It was the same girl who had so much to say at the movies when I was with J. I was debating on ignoring her because I really was having a good time and I didn't want her ruining it.

"I guess ya fat ass didn't hear me," she said even louder this time. Alexa play "move bitch get out the way," I walked right up to her and got in her face, "if you don't get ya bird brain ass on and out of my space I will bash ya head in with one of these bowling balls, play wit me if you want," after I said that she turned on her heels and walked away. I guess she really didn't want no smoke tonight. For the rest of the night me and the girls enjoyed ourselves and that stupid girl didn't come over there again. I went home took a shower and laid down in bed. For some reason I've been thinking about Khai lately so I ended up going to sleep and dreaming about him.

THIRTY-NINE

THINGS HAVE BEEN PRETTY quiet lately. Surprisingly Tyson hasn't been bothering me but usually when he's quiet for too long sooner or later he comes and tries to wreak havoc in my life. I feel like he just sits at home and tries to think of ways to make me miserable but that's not happening. From the looks of it he's moved on so hopefully he's finally done with me. I'm keeping my fingers crossed on that one.

Sometimes you don't understand how much someone can bring drama and negativity in to your life. It's like when your in it things bother you but maybe not so much but once the relationship is over you realize how much trouble the person caused you. Everyday now I am thankful for the peace and quietness in my life. This self love journey has me seeing things in myself that I didn't know were there and learning to love myself more. Because really how can you love someone or expect someone to love you if you can't love yourself.

I've been trying to talk about the things I have experienced and the things I am learning about myself on my blog. If I can help at least one person to learn from anything I've been through then I have accomplished something in life. I've also been making it available for women who have questions or want to share their stories as well. It feels better when you know you're not alone. It's important to have someone to talk to and give advice or just be a listening ear and I'm trying to provide that to women everyday.

There are some days where I feel lonely but I refuse to be one of those women who is with someone out of loneliness. The time for love will come again one day for me and when it does I will definitely be taking my time to get to know someone. Maybe I'll sign up for one of those dating sites just to have someone to talk to or maybe go out on a couple of dates. Nothing too serious though.

I wanted to get some coffee and donuts for the office staff so I left work a little early to stop at Dunkin Donuts. Of course when I get there I see Tyson. I'm really convinced that he's following me or something. It's like the minute I think I'm free from him, he somehow manages to pop up. Not one to be rude I spoke to him when he got closer to me. "Good morning Tyson, how are you?"

"Good morning Kamaya, I'm good. I'm surprised to see you here." I didn't believe what he said at all. He probably was somewhere close and seen me come in here and then tried to act like he wanted something. From what I remember he didn't even like Dunkin Donuts so I know he full of shit or maybe he's getting something for his new girlfriend.

"Well I'm surprised to see you here as well, I thought you didn't like Dunkin Donuts."

"Oh I was just coming to pick something up for a friend, that's all."

Of course he gonna say a friend, you and I both know what that's about.

"That's cool, well I have to go so enjoy the rest of your day." I turned to walk away. Next thing I know he's walking fast behind me.

"Kam hold up, do you think we can go out one day you know for old time sakes."

"I'm sorry Tyson but I don't think that is a good idea. I said to him trying to get into my car. I wanted to get as far away from him as I could. No matter how he tried there was no need for us to talk and there never will be. I already know how the conversation will turn out. Unlocking the car door and right before I slid in he yelled out "Fuck you Kamaya that's why my new bitch is better than ya miserable ass!" Chuckling at him I started my car and hauled ass away from him. She can be better than me and deal with his crazy ass all she wants. If she was that great though then why did he keep bothering me was the million dollar question.

A little while later I arrived at work and the receptionist Michelle let me know I had some type of delivery in my office. I know I didn't order anything so I had no clue what it could have been. Hopefully Tyson didn't send me a bomb or something trying to kill me. He's unstable like that. I went to put the coffee and donuts in the break room then headed to my office.

. . .

Opening the door I immediately noticed a vase with yellow roses in it. I walked over to my desk and smelled them first and then I noticed the card. Picking up the card I was a little nervous because I had no idea who they could be from. The card said, "Miss Kamaya ever since I first saw you all those years ago in Miami I couldn't get you off my mind. Us constantly running into each other is a sign that there is something special between us if you gave it a chance. I got you yellow roses because they signify friendship and I hope we can build one." They were from Khai and he didn't leave a number or anything for me to even say thank you.

I can't believe after all these years he was still trying. I really thought he would have moved on by now. I appreciate that he even wants to have a friendship with me but was I ready for that yet. My guard is so far up that It will be hard for him or any one else to knock it down. I do want to thank him for the roses though but I don't have a number to call him. Oh I know maybe I'll send him one of those sandwiches from the deli. I had to call Gabi and see what she thought about this and did she even know he was sending the flowers since she's been talking to Bane all the time.

After the phone rung a couple of times she picked up. "Hey Kam, I'm guessing your at work and saw those beautiful yellow roses?" She asked. "So you knew and didn't tell me he was sending them?" I asked her.

"Well yeah I know because he asked me what color should he get because he didn't want to do the typical red rose. So I explained to him the significance of the yellow ones and said they were perfect and took it from there. I thought that was sweet of him," she told me.

"Well yes Gabi that was sweet of him but I wasn't expecting

them. I don't know how to take them, like I'm not ready to deal with someone not even on a friendship level. Girl you know Tyson's psychotic ass still keeps bothering me. I don't need Khai getting caught up in no mess with him," I explained to her.

"Girl fuck Tyson and don't let Khai's business suits and laid back manner fool you, trust me Bane done told me some stories and Tyson better be the one who has to worry. Khai is far from a punk honey and Tyson can fuck with him if he wants and he'll get his dumb ass killed. Okkurrt!" She said laughing.

I heard what she was saying but I still was skeptical and the way Tyson was so unstable I'm just not sure. At the same time though I can't put my life on hold for Tyson. "Your right Gab and I will think about it. In the meantime do you think I should send him something just to say thank you since he didn't leave a number or anything?" I asked her.

"Nope, trust he didn't do it to get anything in return just sit there and look at them pretty things and enjoy your day. Trust me you will be hearing from me again and probably soon." She said it like she knew something I didn't and before I got a chance to ask her what she was talking about she hung up on me. Laughing out loud I couldn't believe this trick hung up on me.

I wonder what she meant though about me hearing from him soon. It would be nice to go out with someone other than my girls though. I'm still thinking about setting up an online dating profile. I don't think I'll tell anybody if I did do it especially Keysha because she is totally against online dating. I'm not too sure about it either but my life is a little boring and I could use a little fun.

FORTY

IT'S BEEN a couple of weeks and I haven't heard anything from Khai since he sent the roses. Since he didn't reach out I did end up signing up for a dating site. The first couple of days I just took some time setting up my profile and scrolling through some profiles. There were a couple of handsome guys on there but I didn't reach out to anyone. As I was scrolling I wasn't surprised when I seen Tyson's profile on there. I wouldn't be surprised if he was on there meeting chicks even when we were in a relationship. I feel bad for whoever falls for his shit.

Anyway after about a week or so I started getting messages. Some were interesting and some I had to delete as soon as I saw their pictures. A Lot of these guys were inappropriate too. They would send messages in the middle of the night like that was a way to get dates. Maybe for some of these broads out here but not me. I'm not looking for a relationship but I wanted someone to at least be about something.

There was this one guy Kyle who seemed interesting so I decided to respond to his messages and after talking for about a week we agreed to meet up for dinner. Tonight was the date night and I was so nervous about it. I hope this dude isn't a killer or a rapist or something crazy. Lord knows I don't need anymore crazies in my life. I don't have the time or patience for it. Since I didn't know him we said we would just meet at the place.

Lets just say Kyle was fine you hear me, a little too fine to be single and on some dating site so I know there has to be something with him. He also had a good sense of humor and he kept me laughing until we started asking each other personal questions. I told him about being a mother and starting my own practice. He had a pretty good job but when it came to him telling me about his kids I immediately lost interest. This fool told me he had 9 kids with 7 baby mamas. My eyes damn near fell out of my head when he told me that. Since he was cool besides all the kids and baby mamas, I stayed for the rest of the dinner but best believe he was going on the block list by the end of the night.

Then there was Tony. Tony was also a nice guy at first but once we were out on a date things changed for the worst. "So Kamaya you gonna give me some pussy tonight since I'm paying for this date?" I spit my damn drink out and it almost got on him. He looked to be dead ass serious too and if so he got me all the way fucked up. "No I am not, just because you treated me to dinner doesn't automatically mean I have to fuck you."

"Thats where you're wrong Kamaya, that's exactly what that means, so either you're going to give it up willingly or I'm just gonna take it!" Now I'm sitting here nervous because this nigga really said he would rape me if I didn't give it up. I couldn't even respond to him so I excused myself to go to the bathroom. I had to get away from him for a minute to try and call someone. I went to the bathroom and called Gabi. "Bitch you won't believe what just happened!" I yelled to her as soon as she answered the phone. After telling her everything that happened and where I was I went to use the bathroom.

As I was using the bathroom I heard the door open and I looked down and saw shoes that didn't look like they belonged to a woman. I really started getting nervous and hoped Gabi showed up soon. I texted her quietly to tell her I think Tony came into the bathroom with me.

"Kamaya I know you're in here," he said dragging my name out and knocking on each stall door. "I told you you owe me some pussy so it's time to pay up." I refused to answer because I wanted him to think I came out already but I had no such luck because now he's knocking on the stall door I'm in. He threatened to kick the door down and as soon as he said that I heard the door fly open.

"Aye nigga get the fuck out of here!" I heard a voice yell and I swear it sounded like Khai. Gabi must have called him and I'm glad she did because who knows what would have happened to me. "Nah my man, her fat ass owe me some pussy and Im getting it any way I have to, even if that means I have to take it." Even his voice sounded different and I was scared for me and Khai at this moment. "My dude I don't think you heard me, now you got ten seconds to get the fuck out of here and never see, speak or even think about Kamaya again, is that understood?" Khai asked Tony and Tony agreed and left out the bathroom.

"Sweetheart it's okay to come out now," Khai quietly said to me. I was still a little too nervous to come out. "Um are you sure?" I asked him with a shaky voice. "Yes babygirl I'm sure and I can assure you he won't be bothering you again." I tried to calm my shaking hands down and I came out of the stall and as soon as I did Khai grabbed me and hugged me.

"Khai what are you doing here? How did you know I was here?" I asked him with tears coming down my face. I thought it was bad when Tyson kidnapped me but this was worse because this man was actually going to rape me. At least I knew that Tyson wasn't going to really hurt me. Snapping me out of my thoughts Khai started to answer my question. "Well Gabi was on the phone with Bane when you called her and he knew I was in the area and he called me since I was closer and I'm glad it was me instead of Gabi because who knows what he would have tried to do if I wasn't here."

I really couldn't believe that he came to rescue me like that. I mean I know he was interested in me but I didn't think he would possibly risk his life for me. Anything could have happened to him and I will forever be grateful to him.

"I don't know how to repay you for saving me, I was so scared that he really was going to do something to me," I said to him.

"Shh, shh you're okay now," he said while rubbing my back.

"I know, I mean I've been kidnapped before but never been so close to rape." He stopped rubbing my back and pulled back a little and gave me a surprised look.

. . .

"Yes I've been kidnapped before but that's another story for another day." After another minute the tears finally stopped and I walked over to the sink to wipe my face off and we headed out of the bathroom. "Kamaya please tell me you drove yourself and didn't let that crazy fool know where you live."

The way he said my name had me secretly squeezing my thighs together, the shit sounded so sexy. I shouldn't even be thinking like that after being traumatized but I couldn't help it.

"Yes I drove myself and thank god I did because I would hate if he knew where I lived. Omg I feel so embarrassed now. I can't believe this night turned out like this."

"Listen there is nothing to be embarrassed about, you didn't know it was going to turn out like that and no one is judging you for that especially me."

"Thank you for that and I really appreciate your help tonight and thank Bane for me for even thinking to call you. Oh shit I better call Gabi because I know she's probably losing her mind right now. Oh! Also thank you for the roses, they were beautiful." I told him as we made it my car.

"No need to thank me, anything to put a smile on your beautiful face" he said causing me to blush. After we said goodnight to each other I got in my car and called Gabi. I told her I was staying with her tonight because I really was afraid to go home.

At first I was a little nervous because I wasn't sure if Tony actually left or was waiting around for me and was planning on following me. I drove towards the police station just in case and once I realized I wasn't being followed I headed over to Gabi's. I just wanted to take a bath and forget about this night. I'm glad I had some clothes at her house because that's exactly what I was going to do.

FORTY-ONE

LAST NIGHT WAS SO BAD. For hours I just tossed and turned and when I did manage to fall asleep I kept dreaming about Tony trying to rape me and I would wake up screaming and sweating. The dreams were much worse than what actually happened. In the dream he kicked down the door and would be so close to raping me but then I would wake up. I wish I would have gotten Khai's number because talking to him probably would have helped me sleep. Since I couldn't talk to him I just had inappropriate thoughts about him until I feel asleep.

The next day I decided to stay home from work. Luckily I didn't have that many appointments so I was able to cancel them or have them see someone else for the day. With the way I'm feeling I need to make an appointment for myself. I needed some help because I didn't want to have nightmares every night. I can't imagine what would have happened if he actually would have succeeded. I shuddered just thinking about it.

I got up to see if Gabi was still here and to get some breakfast. When I looked at the time it was already after 10am so I know she went to work already. I got up to handle my hygiene and go down to the kitchen. I made myself an egg and sausage sandwich with a cup of tea. I noticed her laptop on the counter so I grabbed it so I can post on my blog about what happened to me last night. It was important to share that with my followers so they know the possible dangers of online dating.

For the next couple of hours I chatted online with multiple women that had the same thing happen to them or even worse. It's a shame that there were guys out there doing this and using these websites to find their victims. After a while I went on the dating site I was signed up for and quickly deleted my profile. After crazy Tony I was giving up online dating. I would just have to take my chances on meeting someone at the store or something. I don't know about meeting someone in a store either because that's where I met Jamil and look where that got me.

I really didn't have any plans today so I was just going to catch up on some reading and relax. I had so many books on my kindle I didn't even know where to start. I decided to read *Hope* by Iesha Bree. I think she was a dope author who doesn't get the recognition that she deserves. Anyway halfway through the book I hear my phone go off. When I looked at it I noticed it as a unknown number and it made me a little nervous.

305-867-3436: *Good morning beautiful*
  Me: *Good morning, who is this?*
  305-867-3436: *It's Khai, I just wanted to check on you and make sure you were doing okay.*
  Me: *Oh hi, yes I'm good. Thank you for asking. I guess I don't have to ask you how you finally got my number.*
  305-867-3436: *Lol you know ya girl gave it to me but it was all innocent. I'm just making sure you good.*
  Me: *Well thank you, I really appreciate it.*
  305-867-3436: *No problem ma, but I'll let you go. Don't hesitate to use this number if you need anything. Have a good day.*
  Me: *lol maybe I will. Thanks, you have a good day as well.*

I saved his number just in case I need to call him for anything. It was nice of him to check on me like that even though I'm gonna kill Gabi for giving him my phone number without asking me. I guess it won't be so bad going on a date with him since he has been trying to show me attention. I could use a nice date sometime soon.

A few minutes later my phone went off again and this time it was Tyson calling but I didn't answer so of course he kept calling but I sent him right to voicemail. He left a message so I decided to enlighten myself and listened to it. So I'm listening and he claims he misses me and all that other bullshit. He goes on about us being back together and how he wants to do all this shit together. Just some crap that he thinks I want to hear but I really don't.

· · ·

The phone starts ringing again and it's him yet again. I still don't want to be bothered by him so he leaves another message. This time his message was totally different. This time it was fuck you miserable, fat bitch, he's telling me I'm going to be lonely for the rest of my life, blah, blah, blah. This is typical of him. He pretends to miss me and love me but then seconds later he's cursing me out. It's just a repeating cycle with him and he thinks he does nothing wrong.

I was really trying to finish this book so I ended up putting my phone on do not disturb just in case Tyson decided to call again. It's not like I can just block his number because he'll just call from different numbers. Eventually I finished it and it was so good and I figured I'll take a nap.

Hours later I woke and Gabi had made it home from work. I probably should go home soon since Quran is supposed to be bringing Summer Reign home sometime today and I miss my baby. I'll talk to Gab for a little then I'll head out. Walking in the kitchen I smelled the food she was cooking and my stomach immediately started growling. I realized I didn't eat since this morning.

"Hey Kam, I'm frying some chicken do you want some?"

"Hell yeah you know I do," I laughed. "Oh and Gab who the hell told you to give Khai my number?"

"Nobody told me but Kam be honest that man put his life on the line last night so I felt he deserved it." I I guess she did have a point considering he really didn't have to do what he did for me, so I guess I can't be mad at her for that.

"So do you think I should call him or even go on a date with him?"

"As a matter of fact I do Kam, you deserve happiness and you won't find it if you don't give anyone a chance and I think Khai at least deserves a chance."

"Ugh I guess you're right, I'll call him one of these day."

We continued to talk a little while longer while we ate. She told me about her situation with Bane and how they talk everyday and he was planning another trip out here soon. I'm happy she found someone even though he's so far away but hey it's a start. We also talked a little more about Khai and I really got to thinking that maybe I will call him soon and see about possibly going on a date.

Feeling so much better I went back to work the next day. I knew I couldn't stay away from my clients for too long. They needed my help and that's what I was going to do. I got to work and made an appointment for myself with one of the counselors. When I was walking away Michelle stopped me. "Oh Ms. Jones there was a guy named Tony that came by here for you yesterday. He didn't want to leave any information and he didn't want to make an appointment either."

"Thanks Michelle but if he ever comes here again immediately call the police." Now I was starting to worry again because he clearly wasn't going to let this go.

Opening my office door I noticed another set of roses on my desk and this time there were some cream and some pinks one. Picking up the card I began to read it outloud. "Hi Kamaya I got you these two colors because they symbolize thoughtfulness and admiration. I wanted you to know that I was thinking of you and that I admire you for the things you do. Enjoy your day sweetheart~Khai." No one has bought me flowers like this before especially since we aren't even dating but he was making me feel all giddy inside.

· · ·

I picked up the phone to call him before my first client came in because this required a phone call not a text message. Sometimes text messages are so informal. Just as I was about to hang up after the fourth ring his sultry voice sounded like music to my ears.

"Well isn't this a pleasant surprise, I can't believe Miss Kamaya Jones is actually on my line and I didn't have to call her first," he chuckled.

"How are you Khai? I was calling to tell you thank you for the roses, they were beautiful."

"Not as beautiful as you are," he said making me blush.

"Thank you aren't you sweet, but listen I don't want to hold you up, again just wanted to say thank you."

"You can thank me by finally letting me take you out on a date this weekend. How does Saturday sound?" Now I know I said I should give him a chance but now that he's asking me again I'm a little nervous but all I heard was Gabrielle's voice in my head telling me to go for it so that's exactly what I was going to do. "Yes Saturday will be perfect."

"Cool well I will call you sometime this week and we can go over the details, you enjoy the rest of your day miss lady."

"That's cool and you enjoy the rest of your day as well sir." I hung up the phone and I started thinking if I made the right choice or not but there was only one way to find out.

FORTY-TWO

TONIGHT WAS the night of the date and to say I was nervous was an understatement. I wasn't sure where we were going but he told me to dress comfortable. So I decided on some Fashion Nova jeans and a white tee shirt with a long pink duster over it. The weather was kind of warm so I wore some sandals. Thank goodness I just got my toes done and the white polish on them was popping against my dark skin. I didn't feel like doing too much to my hair so I just put it in a high bun with a few little pieces coming down framing my face. I kept my makeup very light, just adding some bronzer and my Chatterbox mac lipstick. Khai was coming around 8 and it was already 7:45 so I had to finish getting myself together.

At 8 o'clock on the dot my doorbell rang so I grabbed my watch off the dresser and headed down to answer the door. Opening the door, Khai was standing there smiling with some jeans on and a blue shirt and some blue, black, and white air max sneakers. He had this nice watch on that looked like it cost a lot of money. "Good evening Miss Kamya, your looking really nice, are you ready to go?"

"Good evening Mr. Khai, your looking nice as well and yes I am ready." I told him while grabbing my bag and keys off the table I had by the door. When we walked outside he had this midnight blue Acura MDX and that thing was shiny as hell. He must have just gotten it washed and waxed.

He walked slightly behind me and guided me to the car and when we got to the car he reached around me and opened the door for me. The inside was soft black leather and it felt so comfortable. When he got in and started it up the radio came on and *Simple Things by Miguel* was playing. This is my favorite song and I can definitely relate to it. That's all I wanted from someone, the simple things. I didn't need the fancy car and all that materialistic stuff, granted they were nice but not needed. I asked him if he can turn it up and I started singing my heart out. Mind you I can't sing worth a damn but I can't listen to this song and not sing.

After the song went off he turned the radio down and looked at me and started laughing. "I'm glad you feel comfortable enough to sing around me but baby that was terrible, he started laughing even harder. "I'm sorry but I can't help it whenever that songs come on, I'm glad I was entertaining." I chuckled. "Baby Girl don't apologize for being yourself and don't let me or anybody else make you feel like you have to," he said matter of factly. "Is the song true though, do you really want the simple things?"

"Yes it's definitely true, I mean things like money, cars, and all that stuff is nice but I want someone that I can be myself with. I like to be able to sing even though I can't, laugh, dance, you know just chill. I'm not a complicated chick at all."

"I can dig it and I feel the same way, you have to be with someone you can be yourself around and not feel like your being judged." For the rest of the ride we just talked about simple things like favorite types of music, our favorite movies and things.

When we got to our destination I got super excited because we were at Top Golf and I always wanted to come here but never got around to it. I was also glad he didn't do the typical dinner and a movie type of date. Now I like dinner and a movie but I think those are cliche types of first dates. He already got some cool points just for stepping out of the box.

He came around and opened the door for me and helped me out of the car. As we were walking he had his hand on the small of my back. "Miss Kamaya I hope your okay with coming here, I wanted to try something different and I figured this may be fun."

"Hell yeah I'm okay with it, I like stuff like this," I said excitedly. He laughed at me because I was really out here like a kid. He just didn't know I'm a big ass kid at heart.

"I'm glad you like it, I've never been here before so this should be fun." It was so cool in there since it was dark outside they had these bright, colorful lights. It was kind of packed but not overly packed. He told me we were going to eat first before we played. Apparently he made a reservation for a bay and it wouldn't be ready for a little bit so we had some time to kill.

. . .

While we were eating we talked about everything from our child-hoods, to past relationships, to future goals. He told me how he wants to get married one day and have children. I never really thought about having more kids but maybe if I found someone worth having one by then maybe I would. My phone kept ringing in my bag and at first I ignored it because it was rude to be on the phone while your on a date. After it rang about three or four times back to back I looked to see who it was since it could have been Quran and he had Summer so I wanted to make sure everything was okay.

Pulling my phone out of my pocket I was mad to see it was Tyson and not Quran. It was a good thing that it wasn't Quran since that meant that everything was okay but Tyson calling me wasn't good. I'm not sure why he hasn't gotten it through his head by now that I don't want anything to do with him and he really should move on. I put the phone back in my bag and tried to ignore it.

After about ten minutes it started to ring again. Khai suggested I should answer it figuring it may be an emergency. I didn't want to tell him that it was just a crazy ex even though he kind of experienced Tyson already. Against my better judgement I answered and come to find out Tyson was right outside. He threatened to come in here if I didn't come outside. Now how do I tell Khai that my psycho ex boyfriend was here somehow on our very first date. Nah I'm not going to tell him I'll just excuse myself from the table.

"I'm sorry Khai can you excuse me for a second?" I looked at him apologetically.

"Sure sweetheart is everything okay? He sounded concerned and I debated on telling him the truth or not and probably should have especially because who knows what kind of mindset Tyson is in but I decided not to. I assured him everything was okay and I got up and went outside.

"Tyson what the hell are you doing here?" I practically screamed at him.

"Girl you think I was going to let you just move on with some other nigga? Nah Kam that shit ain't happening so you might as well go in there and tell homeboy this date is over and leave." This fool is tripping to think that shit was really about to happen. There was no way in hell I was leaving with him. "Tyson please just leave and I won't call the cops and get a restraining order against you." He grabbed me by my throat real tight and whispered in my ear, "I said lets fucking go Kamaya and don't let me repeat myself again." Suddenly he let go and was holding his face because Khai came outside and punched him in the face. They started to fight until the cops arrived and I told them I wanted to press charges against Tyson.

"Kam are you good? You were taking kind of long so I started to think something happened so I came out to check on you and I'm glad I did because he could have really hurt you."

"Khai I'm so sorry about this and I can understand if you want to end the date and never see me again."

"Kamaya I waited too long to finally go on a date with you and now that I have my chance I'm not going to let some fool that obviously can't get over you ruin that for me. So let's go back in here and continue our date. Is that cool?"

"Yes Khai its cool and again I apologize," I sincerely said. "There's no need to babygirl and it's clear that you are worth it since all your exes seem to act crazy over you and have a hard time getting over you." He grabbed my hand and headed back inside and continued to enjoy the rest of our date like nothing ever happened.

FORTY-THREE

FOR THE LAST couple of months things with Khai have been going great. He still sends me different colored roses. Sometimes he'll send other types of flowers or fruit baskets. Yesterday he sent me some sunflowers after I told him how much I loved them. This time around everything between me and him just seemed different. Things just seemed to flow naturally between us. More than it has been with anyone else. I was able to be myself with him and not feel like I was being judged. Like the time we were having a conversation about something and I noticed this squirrel climbing a tree and I told him I wanted to be a squirrel. Instead of thinking I was crazy, he just laughed and entertained my silliness.

We still haven't had sex yet and I'm glad we didn't because sex oftentimes complicates things and I don't want to complicate things with him. Lord knows I want to though because it's been a long time. We have kissed though a few times and whenever we do I get weak in my knees so I can imagine what sex would be like with him. I don't want to rush it but I've been really horny lately so I may just seduce him first.

Every week we go out on a date either Friday or Saturday. Our dates range in different things. Sometimes we have breakfast, some-times lunch, other times it may be dinner. We've been to the movies a couple of times, went back to TopGolf, sometimes we just go for walks. What people don't understand is dates don't always have to cost a lot of money, there are plenty of cheap and free dates if your open to them.

Most of the time he plans the dates which is very refreshing because a lot of dudes don't know how to plan a real date. They think Netflix and chill is the ideal date and maybe for some of these girls maybe it is. Not for me though, I like when a man puts an effort into the date and not try to do things that everybody else does. Your dates should reflect both of your personalities and for two people who just vibe well will have a good time regardless.

Today was date day again and as usual I have no idea where we are going. He never tells me where we are going, he just tells me what kind of clothes to wear. We were doing a daytime date today so who knows where we are doing. It was finally summer and I just got some new maxi dresses so I put a peach colored one on and some sandals that I found on sale. He always picks me up so I was sitting on the porch waiting for him to come. I really enjoyed sitting on porch especially when it was a nice breeze blowing.

Khai arrived and when he got out of the car my juices started immediately flowing. He was wearing some pants with a button up shirt and some shoes. You can tell he just got a haircut and his beard was looking nice. He walked up to me and pulled me out of my chair and wrapped his arms around me and kissed me on my lips. Even a simple peck from him turned me on. He made sure my door was locked and we walked to the car.

Since we've been dating I never had to touch a car door any door handle as long as he was around. It was nice being catered to I mean the others were gentlemen but Khai was on a whole different level. He always opens my door and pulls my chairs out wherever we go. There was still that fear of being hurt but he hasn't giving me a reason to think that he would so I'm just going to go with the flow.

Once we were in the car I started asking questions. "So Khai where are we going today?" Just like any other time he gave me the same answer he always gives me. "Kam I don't know why you ask me every time we go somewhere knowing I'm not going to tell you," he laughed and leaned over and kissed me again. I folded my arms and began to pout. "Don't be over there making that face because the same way it didn't work any other time it's not going to work this time." I just stuck my tongue out at him and turned the radio up.

"Oh so what you turned the radio up so you don't have to hear me talk?" He asked me laughing. I didn't even answer him. I was becoming spoiled and it was all his fault. After a few seconds I started laughing too and this was what we did every week. Ill pretend to be mad and he won't pay it any mind. It was fun for us.

The rest of the ride we talked about how our work week was and everything else that was going on our lives and just the world period. It seemed like no matter what we always had something to talk about. After a while we ended up at some park and I still had no idea about why we were here. He got out of the car and went and got something out of the trunk then came and opened my door.

When I got out I heard music and I saw that he had a picnic basket and a blanket. "Oh my god are we having a picnic?" I got excited because we all know I love food and I also loved picnics. I think picnics are intimate and was nice that he took the time for this.

"Yes baby we are having a picnic and are going to enjoy this jazz concert. I even made the food myself." He sounded so proud when he said that. All this time we've been dating he has never gotten around to cook for me so I was looking forward to his food. We walked for a little bit and found an area fairly close to the stage and put the blanket down and then helped me down on to it.

The food he made was good. We had grilled chicken, potato salad and some fruit salad. To drink we had a bottle of Sauvignon Blanc and some water.The jazz concert was put on by local musicians in the area but it was good. It turned out to be a great day. The sun was shining and it was warm out but not too hot. The concert went on for a couple of hours and I was starting to feel tipsy a little.

It was getting dark out by the time it was over so we ended going back to my place and watch a movie or something on Netflix. We ended up watching *Drug Lords* which is a pretty interesting series on Netflix. After a couple of episodes I felt like I can become a drug lord. We started to get hungry again so we ordered a pizza and had some more wine. The more I drank the more I wanted to have sex so I figured tonight was going to be the night.

See one thing Khai hasn't experienced yet was drunk Kam and drunk Kam says whatever. "Khai I want to know what that mouth do," I whispered seductively. I probably should have waited to say that because he was taking a sip of his drink when I said it and spit it out on the table and began to choke. "My bad baby I didn't mean to make you choke," I giggled while patting his back. "Damn ma you caught me off guard with that but you ain't said nothing but a word." He then picked me up and carried me to my room. All I'm going to say is after tonight Khai has become the best lover I ever had.

He ended up staying the night for the first time it was cool. I got up first so I made breakfast and we just chilled out. It was definitely something I can get used to but not too soon. He left because he had to do something to get ready for the work week and I wanted to clean up before Summer Reign got home. We said our goodbyes and left.

I realized I ran out of the bathroom and kitchen cleaner so I threw on some leggings with my shirt and some slides to run to Walmart. When I got in the car I hooked my phone up to the car so I can call Gabi. I had to tell her about the magical night I had with Khai. As soon as she answered the phone I immediately started telling her what happened. "Girl let me tell you, Khai damn near sucked my uterus out and it was the best ever!" "Well damn I guess the saying is true, birds of a feather flock together cause honey Bane is the same way," she laughed. "Listen girl I think I'm in lo..., the next thing I know I'm trying to step on the brakes and they aren't working and I was going down a small hill so the car just was going down the hill on its own and the last thing I remember was hearing Gabi call my name as the car hit a tree and I blacked out.

FORTY-FOUR

WAKING up to the sounds of beeping, it took me a minute to fully open my eyes and realize I was in a hospital. I tried to sit up but my head felt like it weighed a ton. When I tried to open my mouth I felt something in my throat. Looking over to my left I saw Gabi sleeping in a chair and there were multiple vases of flowers and teddy bears around the room. I wonder who the hell could have sent all of these.

I was hoping Gabi woke up soon or someone came into the room because I really had no clue as to why I was here. The last thing I remember was Khai being at my house and that's it. Everything else after that is blur. I started to feel pain in my right leg and I noticed a cast on it. The tears slowly came down my face partially because of the pain and also because I had no clue as to what happened which was scary. If I can't remember why I'm here what else did I forget.

"Hello Ms. Jones it's nice to see you awake," a nurse lowly spoke to me. At the same time Gabi started to wake up and when she looked at me she screamed, "OMG Kam you're awake!" The nurse continued to check me out and she said she was going to go get the doctor so they can take the tube out of my mouth.

When she left the room Gabrielle came over and sat on the bed with me. "Kamaya you gave us all a good scare. You've been out for like two days." I couldn't believe I was here and out for that long. I wonder what happened to my breaks to go out like that. Where is my daughter? Has anyone went and checked on my dog? I had so many questions. Gabi must have read my mind because she assured me that Summer was good and with Quran and they had been up here and that she went and made sure Gucci got fed and went out for his walks. This was exactly why she was my best friend.

A few minutes later the nurse came back and she was accompanied by a doctor. "Hello Ms. Jones, I'm Dr. Brown and we are going to get that tube out of you okay." His voice was so soothing. "Now when we take this out your throat is going to be a little sore so I'm going to need you to drink plenty of water, but slowly and try not to talk too much okay." I just nodded my head since I couldn't answer. "On the count of three I want you to cough, 1.2.3." and as I coughed he pulled that awful tube out of my throat. He went on to explain to me that when I crashed I had a traumatic brain injury from hitting my head on the steering wheel and its possible to have some slight memory loss but it shouldn't last too long and I broke my right leg and I will probably have to go to rehab when I get out of here. The tears started again. He apologized and left the room taking the nurse with him.

So far I couldn't think of anything that I may have forgotten except why I was here. Gabrielle gave me some water to drink and it felt good going down my throat. "Kam honey do you remember anything that happened?" I just shook my head no because I had no clue. She went on to explain to me that we were on the phone and my car wouldn't stop and I hit a tree. I can't even think about where I was going. She told me I was by myself and I was glad that Summer wasn't in the car with me because who knows what would have happened to her.

"Kamaya I have some bad news for you," she grabbed my hand before she started talking again. "Honey the police said it looks like someone was tampering with your brake lines and that's what cause you to crash, so someone was trying to kill you." I looked at her with a shocked expression and the tears started yet again. Like who the hell would try and kill me. Gabi speaking again snapped me out of my thoughts. "Kam do you think Tyson would do something like that?" She voiced concerningly. I would hope he wouldn't but the way he has been I wouldn't put it past him.

"To be honest Gab I'm not even sure of what he's capable of these days, it's not like he hasn't threatened me before, I just never thought that he would ever go through with it. "Well Kam I think it was him because I don't see anyone else doing something like that to you. The police came by here and they left a card for you to call them if you have any ideas of who could have done this. I really thought about what she said and I hate to accuse him if he didn't do it but at the same time he has done so much to me that he needs to pay for everything he has done. I'm going to think about it some more and probably give them a call later or tomorrow. Gabi told me that's she's been there since I got there so now that I was awake she was going to go home for a little bit. The pain medicine they gave me was catching up to me and I was getting sleepy so I said goodbye to her and went to sleep as soon as she walked out the door.

When I woke up it was dark in the room so I must have been out for a while. I'm not even sure if the nurse or anybody came back in the room. I was starting to feel hungry so I was going to call the nurse to see if I can get some food but before I got a chance to reach for the button I noticed a figure sitting in the chair. They had a hood on so at first I couldn't recognize who it was until he sat up to speak and I became nervous.

"Hello Kamaya, surprised to see your still alive," his voice sounded different, it was actually kind of creepy. "What do you mean you're surprised to see me alive? My voice was trembling. It sounds like he's admitting he tried to kill me. Why would he do that though? I mean what would be the point of killing me, hell he couldn't even be with me if I was dead.

"I thought for sure you would have died when I cut those brake lines, but here you are so I guess I have to try something else."

"Wh..Why would you want to kill me?" I nervously asked.

"It's simple Kam I told you if I can't have you then no one can and since you called yourself trying to move on I have to kill you because I can't see you with no one else." He said it like it was something normal to say. I figured if I keep talking to him I can either sneak and press the nurse button or someone would just come in.

"Tyson if I did then you wouldn't be able to be with me either so would what would be the point of you killing me?"

"Oh that's simple too, when I kill you then I'll kill myself and we can be together in heaven," Now I know I said that I thought he was bipolar or something but this nigga is bat shit crazy.

Next thing I know he walked over to the bed and tried to put something over my face but the nurse walked in. "Sir what are you doing?" "Oh nothing, I was just making sure she was comfortable" he sounded so convincing. I gave her a look like he was lying so she stayed there for a couple minutes longer than she needed to. Once he noticed she wasn't leaving he told me he would come back another day. I hope he doesn't but I was definitely going to call these police officers.

FORTY-FIVE

IT'S BEEN a few months since the whole Tyson killing me incident and my short hospital stay. I did forget a few things but it didn't last long. I just got my cast removed not that long ago so I was able to fully walk again. The whole time I was down, Khai was there for me every single day. He made sure I was taken care of and wanted for nothing. There isn't a day that goes by that he doesn't send me some type of flower or fruit basket or whatever else he can think of. Quran and

Tati have been super helpful with Summer. They both have been coming by to help out with her and making sure she got to and from school everyday. I may not like what they did to me but its all in the past and the three of us co-parent well together. The children are more important than any problems we had.

Today we are going out on a double date with Gabi and Bane. He's in town for a little while so it will be nice to hang out with them. I finally know where we are going ahead of time only because Gabi told me, Khai sure wasn't going to. We decided to go Dave and Busters so we can eat and drink and go bowling. Maybe I'll get them to play some games too. I think this will be a fun night.

Ever since I came home from the hospital Khai has been staying at my house a couple times out of the week. Whenever he did he would get up and make me breakfast and usually feed me breakfast in bed. On the tray would be little love notes. It was so cute and thoughtful. Today I got up before him so I decided to try and return the favor. As I was making the eggs I felt some arms wrap around my waist. So much for trying to serve him breakfast in bed. "Good morning baby," he said kissing me on my cheek. "Good morning handsome," I turned around to hug and kiss him. He was standing looking all good with some grey sweatpants on a white tee and I was ready to say fuck this breakfast and give him something else for breakfast.

"Ma why you looking at me like that," he smirked. I couldn't help but to bite my bottom lip. "Oh nothing, breakfast should be ready soon." I turned back around to finish cooking. "Kamaya come here baby," when I walked over to him he pulled me down onto his lap. "Fuck that breakfast ma, right now I need some of that sweet stuff between them legs," he said rubbing on my thighs. Next thing I know he picked me up and carried me to the bedroom. Luckily he turned the stove off before we went in there or them damn eggs would have burned.

By the time we left out of the room again it was time to get ready to go out. We both went in the kitchen to clean up what I left behind when I was attempting to make breakfast and we got in the shower again and of course we had to go another round. At the rate we are going we might not make it out of here on time.

After about twenty minutes in the shower we finally got out to get dressed for real this time. I noticed Gabi called me a couple of times and Bane called him so we were definitely running late. We both got dressed in some jeans and tee shirts with some sneakers. Today was all about comfort. If I had it my way I was gonna kick all their asses in bowling and anything else we decided to play. I can be very competitive when it comes to games.

We ended up staying there for hours and it was such a good time. I ended up beating them at multiple games and when it was boys against the girls, Gabi and I beat them each time. I'm thinking they did that shit on purpose. Gabi and Bane were so cute together and I wish he lived closer because he was good for her. I found out he was a single father to a set of 5 year old twins. I wondered what happened to their mother. I can't imagine not being around my child for too long. After we had a few drinks we all went our separate ways and agreed on doing something together again before Bane went back home.

Neither Khai or I wanted to go back home yet so we decided to take a drive around town. There was this hill that you can go up and see the stars so we decided to do that. I was a little tipsy so it was a bitch climbing that hill but we made it. Khai had a blanket in the car so we laid the blanket down and watched the stars for a while. It was quiet and it was a clear night so the stars were shining extra bright tonight.

As we laid there he grabbed my hand and began talking to me. "Kam these last few months have been nothing short of amazing. You are amazing and so beautiful. You have been through so much and still continue to be strong. I know I told you this before but I am proud of you and I am proud to call you my girl and one day I will be proud to call you my wife. I love you Kamaya Jones," he leaned over and kissed me on my lips. This was the first time he told me he loved me. I knew I loved him but I was still a little afraid to say it. In my heart I knew he was the one but there was still that little doubt of him hurting me like everyone else even though until this day he hasn't giving me a reason to think otherwise. He must have sensed my apprehension because he looked at me and said, "Kamaya you don't have to say it back if you don't feel comfortable."

"Khai it's not that it makes me uncomfortable it's just that I'm scared. I do love you and you have been there for me more than anyone ever has and I definitely appreciate you. Everything about this makes me scared though. I'm afraid one day you may realize you don't want me anymore and I don't think I can take another heart-break." I didn't want to cry but the tears just started flowing out of my eyes. He began to wipe my tears, "baby I understand how you feel but trust me when I tell you Kam I'm not those other niggas and I would never in my life hurt you. I will be here for you until my dying day and always treat you like the queen that you are. I started crying even harder. Looking him in his eyes, I told him how much I loved him and asked to him to never hurt me. "I promise Kamaya I will never hurt you." And for the rest of the night he made love to me under the stars like he never has before.

Since that night we told each other we loved each other things have gotten even better. He's everything I never knew I needed. Even him and Quran get along. They met when I was in the hospital and at first Khai wasn't feeling him or Tati because of what they did to me but he tolerated him because he was Summer's dad and he knew he wasn't going anywhere. Khai was also good with Summer. He treated her like she was his own child and it made me think about giving him a child one day. I know he would make an amazing father. Just like him and I have date night we also take Summer somewhere every week. Today we were going to get ice cream and go to Barnes and Noble. My baby was just like me, she loved ice cream and reading.

The day turned out to be a good one and I was so happy that Khai and Summer had the relationship that they had. Sometimes at night after I would give her a bath, Khai would go in and read to her or let her read to him. Whenever he's here she doesn't even let me do it anymore. Its cool though because I rather have her like him than don't. Even though she was younger when Tyson was around, you can tell she really didn't like him. I noticed a while ago she didn't like too many people but she loved herself some Khai.

Khai came into the room with some basketball shorts on and a wife beater, as always he was turning me on without trying. "Well she's out like a light, tonight she wanted to read so tonight she read *Princess for Hire by Kimberley M*, it was cute," he said laughing.

"Oh yeah she loves that book, she reads it everyday." He just laughed and went to take a shower.

While he was in there I turned on the news. I tried to keep up with what was going on in the world. "Tonight we have news of a house fire on Inglewood Ave and there seemed to be one person in there that perished in the fire. The victim's name is Tyson Lattimore and it looks like he was the only one in the house at that time. The police are doing an investigation on what was the cause of the fire. Now to John with the weather." I turned the tv on and sat there in shock when I heard that, I couldn't believe that Tyson was dead. I know I wanted him to leave me alone but I didn't wish death on him. I shed a tear or two because despite everything I did love him at one point. I did feel sorry for his family though.

FORTY-SIX

IT'S BEEN two years since Khai and I made things official and it has been the best two years of my life. To this day we have never had a single argument. We have had some disagreements but it was about simple stuff. We always made sure we never went to bed angry with each other. The communication we had with each other was wonderful. I never felt I had to be something I wasn't. Everything about our relationship was genuine. Being with Khai made me question every other relationship I was in. I think I loved the others but Khai was my soulmate.

When I'm around him I just feel a sense of peacefulness and calmness like nothing I ever experienced. He still always sends me different types of flowers and at least once or twice a week he sends me and my staff lunch. We still make sure we have our date nights and when we do we disconnect from everyone else in the world and we always try to leave work stuff at work and focus on each other on our dates. I think that's an important part in our relationship. Often-times people lose sight of each other and that sometimes causes a strain on their relationship.

Quran and Tati ended up having another baby. It seems like she gets pregnant every year. I lost track of how many they have now. Summer loves being a big sister. So far I haven't been pregnant but we did have a scare once. Honestly it wouldn't be a bad thing to have a baby with Khai. This time though I would like to be married before I have another baby. Speaking of marriage we have talked about it but he hasn't asked me yet so who knows when it will happen but I am ready though. This one I am certain about. Khai has not given me a reason to question anything about him.

Tonight was girls night and we were just going to meet up at Gabi's house. I missed my girls. We all have so much going on so we didn't get to talk to each other too much but we tried to have girls night at least once a month. Even though I no longer disliked Tati we never invited her back in our circle. Pulling up to Gabi's house I grabbed the bottle of wine I brought and locked up my car. Since we were staying in I just had on some sweatpants and a hoodie since it was cold outside. I used to my key to get into the house. All three of us still had keys to each other's house.

"Hello ladies," they both were sitting on the floor with a glass of wine already. "Damn y'all getting the party started early huh, let me go get me a glass." We were going to order some pizza and wings and just catch up and chill out. Even though I loved Khai and loved spending time with him, it was nothing like spending time with my girls. They help ease my mind when doubts start to creep in.

"So Kam how are things with Khai?" Keysha asked me. "Oh girl they are fucking amazing, I couldn't ask for a better boyfriend but you know I still get nervous like something is going to go wrong. Considering that Quran was good for the first two years until I caught him with Tati, me, and Khai are at the two year mark already.

They both looked at me like I had two heads or something. "Bitch!" Gabi yelled. "Now you know damn well Khai ain't on no fuck boy shit and I will stab you if you ever compare Khai to Quran again." Gabi and Keysha were definitely team Khai. "Damn Gab okay. Anyway what's going on with you and Bane?"

"Girl nothing, we decided things weren't going to work out with the distance and it's hard for him to leave his kids for too long."

"Aww honey I'm sorry it didn't work out with you guys." "Chile it's all good, I'm good." Gabi can fool someone else but her ass wasn't fooling me and I know it affected her more than she tried to claim. She was quick to change the subject too. For the rest of the night we just ate, drank, and laughed. No matter what I knew these two would always have my back.

It was now date night and apparently Khai had something different planned for the day. I woke up to an empty bed but there was a note on his pillow. "Good morning sweetheart today is a special day so I want you to get up and go eat your breakfast that's in the microwave and I will see you tonight. Love K. "I wondered why today was more special than any other date night but I guess I'll find out sooner or later. I got up to handle my hygiene and I noticed another note on the mirror. "I knew you would come here first, I just wanted you to know you are the most beautiful woman in the world." Blushing I put the note on the counter and brushed my teeth so I can go eat.

Walking into the kitchen I noticed some multicolored roses on the kitchen counter. Picking up the card it smelled like Khai. "Kamaya, there are actually no words to describe everything that I feel for you. I am not equipped with such vocabulary, but general terms such as love and infatuation only tickle the feeling. I don't know how I got this lucky but I know that you are MINE. ~Khai". At this point the tears started. He wonders how he got so lucky but I wonder how I got so lucky. This man never ceases to amaze me.

Getting myself together I went to heat up the food in the microwave and there was another note on the microwave. "No matter what you will always be the prettiest girl in the world but today I want you to get pampered. Get your hair, nails, and feet done. I left my card on the dresser for you." ~Khai. So now I get to go get pampered and on his dime. I'm starting to wonder where we are going.

After I ate my breakfast I got up and went to throw on some clothes so I can head out to the salon. I went and got my nails and feet done. Since Khai loves how white polish looks on me I got it on my feet and my nails. Then I went and got my hair done and I think I was finally ready to switch it up so I told my stylist to surprise me with a new style.

Leaving the hair salon I felt like nothing can go wrong today. My hair was cut in layers and it was curly and framed my face a little. I can't wait until Khai saw it, I hope he likes it. I love it so I know he will. Before I left the hair shop there was another note left there for me. "Kam you have changed my life for the better the last couple of years and tonight I'm going to change yours."~K

Now I'm really curious as to what is going on tonight for him to say he's going to change my life. Maybe tonight is the night where he's going to propose. Or maybe he got us the house we talked about getting. We both decided that we would find a new house together. Either way I feel like tonight is going to be epic and I can't wait for it. Let me call Gabi and see if she knows what's going on.

"Hey Kam what's up" she said picking up the phone. "So do you know what's going on tonight? Khai said something about changing my life, do you have any clue as to what he means?"

"Nope Kam I know nothing and shouldn't you be getting ready, bye," she laughed and hung up.

Well she was no help, I walked in the house and there was a big box with a bow on the couch and there was another note attached to it. "To my love, I want you to wear this tonight and there will be a car that will pick you up at 7pm on the dot. I can't wait to see you tonight. Love Khai.

I opened the box expecting a dress or something but nope it was a Quinn Cook jersey, some ripped jeans and a pair of Jordan's. Now to some of y'all this may not seem like much but to me it was. See Khai and I were big Golden State Warriors fans and I loved me some Quinn Cook so I was excited. I know they are playing tonight so maybe we are going to their game. Wait I don't know how we would be going because they are playing in California and we are far from California.

I didn't want to waste too much time dwelling on where we were going so I went to take a quick shower and put on my clothes. At 7 on the dot my doorbell rang and there was this guy with a suit on. "Good evening Miss Jones, I will be your ride for the evening." Wow Khai is getting real fancy tonight with a car service.

The guy helped me into the car and after a while I noticed we were heading towards the airport but I had no clue as to why. We bypassed the normal passenger area and ended up on a private strip area. Standing there next to the stairs of a jet was Khai. He had on a Steph Curry jersey some jeans and the same Jordan's that I had on. Even dressed so casual he looked good. He met me halfway and pulled me into his arms.

"Good evening beautiful, I know it's been a long day for you but it's not over yet. We walked up the stairs of the jet and to my surprise Gabi, Keysha , and Summer were there and they all had on Golden State gear too. "Khai honey what's going on? What are they doing here and why are we all dressed like we are going to a basketball game?" "Because mommy we are going to a game," Summer said matter of factly like I was supposed to know. "She's right baby so sit down so we can get there on time."

So apparently Khai knew someone who had their own plane and we were flying out to California for the Warriors game. I couldn't believe it that we were going to a live game. Since Khai and I have been together we have watched all of their games so actually going to one was going to be so dope.

A few hours later we arrived and went straight to the arena. Walking in I couldn't believe I was at a Warriors game and in Cali at that. This was my first time in California and I hope we had time to explore. After we stopped and got snacks and drinks we headed to our seats and we were practically sitting courtside. I know he had to pay a pretty penny for these tickets.

During the first half of the game Khai kept telling me that he loved my hair. I'm glad he did because I sure wasn't going to change it. After the first half the Warriors were up so we all were feeling good about that. I'm so glad my girls and Summer got to experience this with me. They had a pretty decent halftime show and they had different messages going across the jumbotron. I was reading it when I noticed my name on it. Now why the hell would my name be on there. Summer noticed it too and told me to read it. When I looked at it again it said Kamaya Jones will you marry me? I looked over and Khai was down on one knee.

Of course I started to cry, it seems like I've been doing that alot with Khai but they are always tears of joy. Everyone's attention was on us, even the camera for the jumbotron. I looked at Khai and saw his eyes look a little watery like he was going to cry, then he began to speak. "Kamaya when I first laid eyes on you I knew you were the one for me. I even got snatched off a barstool just for talking to you but I would do it again if I had to. You don't realize the joy that you and Summer bring into my life. I love you both with all my heart and I promise I will love you both until I take my last breath and even death won't my stop my love for you. I told you earlier I was going to change your life tonight, so Miss Kamaya Jones will you do the honor of becoming my wife? I was crying so hard all I could do is shake my head yes. He put the ring on me and lifted me from the seat and kissed me with so much passion. The whole arena erupted in cheers and clapping. The Warriors went on to win the game and I became someone's fiance.

EPILOGUE

1 Year Later

WHEW WHAT A JOURNEY this has been. I've been cheated on, lied to, kidnapped and almost killed but somehow, some way, I survived it all and is going to be marrying my soulmate tomorrow. There were times where I wanted to give up on love but I'm glad I didn't. Who would have thought some random dude I met on vacation with my boyfriend at the time would be the love of my life and the man that I would spend the rest of my life with. I sure didn't, hell at the time I thought J was going to be that guy but obviously that wasn't happening. Even though Quran, Jamil, and Tyson all hurt me I wouldn't go back and change it. They each taught me something about love and to be honest they all prepared me for my true love.

It was hard letting Khai in but he was persistent and I'm so glad he didn't give up on me. It took us years and other relationships to get here but that is how it was supposed to be. If we would have gotten together any soon than it may have not worked out. We both had to go through some things to be prepared for each other. My advice to anyone is don't let a failed relationship get you, just know that is preparing you for the right person.

There are lessons to be learned from my story and I hope at least one person learns something from this. It's hard to know when someone isn't genuine but ladies we really have to be more careful with who we let in our lives, hell men should be more careful too. Some people are energy suckers and when you learn someone is trying to suck the life out of you get as far away from them as you can. Nobody and I mean nobody is worth your sanity and peace.

As far as those guys surprisingly Quran and Tati are still together and they may or may not be having another child. I guess they are working on a football team. With the help of counseling Jamil and his wife are also doing good. Him and I will text each other every few months just to say hi and check on each other. We all know Tyson unfortunately met his demise. Sometimes I still can't believe it. My girls are still around and they aren't going anywhere. Keysha is still with her dude and Gabi has been dating but nothing serious. Bane does ask about her every time he talks to Khai and I'm around.

Enough about all of them. Tonight was my bachelorette party but to be honest I really didn't want anything too over the top. I know Gab and she'll try to have strippers and shit but I didn't want any. Let's see if she listens. Khai rented us a party bus since I had some friends from college coming and of course all the girls from my office was going to be there. We all were just going to go to Fetish and rent out a VIP section and just have a good time.

It was always a good time with these girls no matter where we went. Since it was my last night as a single woman I wanted to have a good time and I was going to do just that. All the fellas were going out somewhere so we all met up at my house and were getting on the bus from there. Everybody arrived and was gonna pregame a little before we left but I wasn't going to drink anything, of course Keysha noticed.

Sounding concerned, Keysha asked me why I wasn't drinking. The reason why is because for the last couple of weeks I've been feeling sick and I'm not sure if I'm pregnant or not. "Well Keysha I'm not drinking because I might be pregnant but I haven't taken a test." They all started to scream. "Calm down, I'm probably not though so don't get all excited."

"There is a way to find out right now," Lisa said. She was one of the girls from my office. We all looked at her like she was crazy because who just walks around with a pregnancy test. "Don't judge me, here Kam take the test," she said as she handed me the test.

I went into the bathroom to take the test and left the bathroom and went in the living room with them. I was nervous about being pregnant. I knew Khai wanted us to have a baby together but I was still nervous. After about five minutes Gabi got up to get the test and she came back in the living room with this big ass smile on her face. I already knew that it was positive just by her smile. "I'm going to be an aunty again!" She came over and hugged me. Then one by one all the girls came and congratulated me and hugged me. I guess I'll tell Khai tomorrow before the wedding. After we calmed down we heard a knock on the door and it was the party bus driver. "Well ladies let's go celebrate my last night as a single lady," I told them and we all walked out the door. All night long we partied and partied hard. I couldn't ask for a better group of friends and I can't wait to marry my best friend tomorrow.

The Next Day

Waking up the next morning I was still surrounded by my girls. Some of them were going to be in the wedding and some were just going to be in attendance but they all wanted to stay and help me get ready. I noticed a vase with sunflowers and there was a card sitting next to it. "To my dearest Kamaya, today you will make me the happiest man in the world and I can't wait to see you walk down the aisle. -Love your husband Khai." My husband, I can't believe in a couple of hours I will be someone's wife. I laid there for a few more minutes and let that thought sink in.

All the girls started to wake up so we had breakfast and began to get ready for today's events. The closer it got to the wedding the more nervous I became. Gabi must have noticed my nervousness because she came over and started rubbing my back. "Kamaya Jones I know your not over there worrying about marrying that man, he worships the ground you walk on so get your head of out your ass and get ready!" "Yes mother," I laughed. Gabrielle always was a little harsh but sometimes I needed that. "In all honesty though Gab what if he decides one day he doesn't want me to be his wife anymore?" I was trying not to cry but I really was nervous.

"Kamaya you deserve all the happiness you have and will continue to have. Khai isn't going anywhere and you and I both know that so dry your eyes because I see the tears threatening to fall and go marry that man." I knew she was right so I just shook off those nervous jitters and got myself together.

―――――

Two hours later and it was finally time to get married. I wasn't a traditional girl so I wasn't going to have a traditional wedding. Instead of a normal white dress I wore a white cocktail style dress with some yellow converses. My bridesmaids all had on some type of yellow cute dresses but they all had on black converses. Khai had on a white suit with a yellow bowtie and some yellow converses as well and the groomsmen wore black suits with the yellow converses. Khai and I both like yellow and it represented the sun and the sun represented a new beginning. Today was the beginning of a new life for us so that's why we chose yellow and it looks good on my skin.

My dad walked me down the aisle and when I reached Khai I couldn't help to start crying. He looked so handsome standing there and I saw that he had tears in his eyes. He mouthed to me, you look beautiful baby and I started blushing. We decided to prepare our own vows and I was going to somehow work in there the fact that I was pregnant.

"Kamaya you have made me the luckiest and happiest man in the world. You give me peace in a world that's full of chaos. I vow to protect you, love you, and provide for you until they put me six feet under. I'm so happy you gave me the honor of taking a chance on me and allowing me to love you and I can't wait to spend the rest of my life with you."

"Khai, I don't know how you did it but you found your way into my heart that was cold and made it warm again. You gave me hope when I had completely lost it. You have become my protector, provider, confidant, lover, and best friend and I know you will be a wonderful second dad to Summer but also to our little boy or girl," he looked at me sideways. "Kam are you telling me your pregnant?" He asked excitedly. "Yes Khai I'm pregnant," and he picked me up and started kissing me. The pastor cleared his throat and began to speak. Congratulations and by the powers vested in me and the state of New Jersey I now pronounce you Mr. and Mrs. Khai Carmichael.

The End

ABOUT THE AUTHOR

Monae Nicole was born and raised in Trenton,NJ, where she lived before moving to Austin, Texas in 2016 with her daughter LaShay. Her love reading begun when she was 14 years old and by the age of 16 she began writing short stories and poems. In 2017 the idea of writing a book was suggested by a good friend resulting in the birth of A Journey To Love! Thank you for taking a chance on me and I hope you enjoy my spin on this tale of love and hope.

f

CPSIA information can be obtained
at www.ICGtesting.com
Printed in the USA
LVHW031823230419
615253LV00003B/473